PRAYERS OF THE DEAD

A MEDIEVAL MYSTERY

PRISCILLA ROYAL

In loving memory of Sharon Kay Penman

The medievals would say there is a new angel carrying a torch in the night sky. We now call those lights stars.

The smaller the mind, the greater the conceit.

— ıAesop, "The Gnat and the Bull", Fables

CONTENTS

1

Eda, Countess of Ness, hated this ugly chapel, Tyndal Priory in general, and England in principle.

Clutching her fur-lined robe closer against her body to mitigate the biting chill of the East Anglian winter air, she decided that the cold in Scotland might be severe but never this barbaric.

She gritted her teeth, tilted her head in preparation to suitably ponder God's glory, and began to gaze heavenward. But as she did, her eyes caught sight of the moss-encrusted window just above the altar.

What blasphemous neglect!

How could the priory monastics fail to clean that window? God's light must fully illuminate the chapel. How shallow their devotion must be, she grumbled. As for the failure of their prioress to recognize the need, she had no words to express her contempt. If she were the prioress of this dismal place, she would have chastised the monastics for allowing the altar window to become so fouled. Ridding it of the vile moss must be of the highest importance. It did not matter if the moss was frozen to the glass or that fingers might be wounded in chipping the defilement away.

Yet she knew there was little point in bringing the omission to anyone's attention. Lack of discipline and incompetence must be expected from an Order that defied God's rules, indeed nature itself, and allowed a woman to lead men.

She took a deep breath and forced herself to set these troubling concerns aside. She was, after all, here to pray and now knelt on the icy stones. The rough floor hurt her knees despite the thickness of her clothes, but she was a woman of deep faith. Enduring a little pain served to remind God of her great devotion. She smiled with a look of determined adoration and now contemplated the body of her Savior hanging from the cross. Musing on that tormented body had always brought her comfort.

This time, however, that twisted figure over the altar did not delight. Instead, a bolt of stinging dread shot through her. Her Savior's eyes were no longer half-closed with his approaching death but seemed to look down at her with burning rage.

Was it the Judgment Day and she had somehow angered him? She whimpered with terror. From church wall paintings, she knew that look meant the condemned soul would soon be stripped naked and fed to jagged-toothed monsters.

Instinctively, she shuffled backwards and looked around, but there was no one else near who might be the object of such damnation. Glancing up again, she knew full well that the ire was directed at her.

How could this be?

She clutched the heavily jeweled cross around her neck and raised it like a shield. In the dull light, the gems flickered with a muddy hue.

Sweating, Eda sat back on her heels and bowed her

head, not out of worshipful devotion,l but to avoid the intense glare of the man on the cross.

The gesture failed. She felt his anger burn through her hood and sear her scalp with holy fire.

Eda cringed, knowing she must have offended God in some way. But how? Did they not have a pact? Surely God had not abandoned the agreement she had made with Him? Hadn't she been true to their bargain? Had she not been faultlessly dedicated for many years to exposing the sins of the wicked?

Bringing punishment to the most egregious miscreants had been her particular crusade. One man had even been assassinated later for his crimes by his victims and that deed had earned favor with many ranking high in the Church, although that was an opinion spoken only in private. Another had committed self-murder. His soul had rightly gone to Hell. Was she not ridding the world of evil? And because of her work, God had agreed to forgive her own greatest sin and allow her to keep it secret. She was unable to comprehend what could have changed to put her in such disfavor.

Suddenly, she knew the cause for His ire!

It must have begun when she came to England, a land of wicked men and suspect Christians. Like a fool, she had agreed to accompany her sinful husband this once. That was her tragic mistake!

The reason she had done so was the fault of that Spanish wife of the arrogant English king. She was displeased by Eda's failure to ever accompany her husband to court. Queen Eleanor did not approve of adulterous or other evil couplings. When she noted that the Earl of Ness never brought his wife to England, she feared he might be tempted by adultery.

Eda's lips twisted in contempt. As if her husband needed

distance from her to wallow in infamy. But he had begged her to comply this one time and had offered to donate to her favorite abbey if she did. She had agreed, concluding that she would make sure the amount was high enough to buy her corpse a burial close to the abbey altar.

As a result of this unpleasant journey, she had failed to promptly expose recently discovered sins, which was her custom. In normal circumstances, she would report her findings to her own bishop in Scotland, a holy man who praised her highly for them. Her secret revelations made him look gifted with divine knowledge when he revealed them during sermons, and she was content with the anonymity because it was more important to have a bishop on her side with God.

She might reveal the secrets here to local churchmen, of course, but they were unknown men, and she did not trust them. They were English and likely possessed of imperfect faith. Her own saintly bishop saw matters as she did, and thus she had decided to wait to reveal her new discoveries until she returned home.

But surely He would forgive her the delay because she had been forced into this journey. Two of Satan's minions she had recently unmasked deserved terrible punishments. Her own maid was one although, if her bishop recommended it, Eda might plead for the woman's life. As a mercy for the woman's devoted service to her, Eda thought it might be sufficient if the maid only lost her hands and was then allowed to beg on the streets. The other was the priest she had trusted for years because her brother, a saintly crusader who had been vilely murdered after his return home, had sworn the man was holy.

She shook her head. How clever the Prince of Darkness was to fool a man like her brother. The priest, she was now aware, exemplified wickedness. As soon as she was back in

Scotland, she would reveal these crimes to her bishop, who would make sure these two foul creatures did not escape a proper punishment. Surely God would not remain angry long over these short delays. God was reasonable.

But there was still the matter of her husband. That, she forced herself to admit, was more likely the cause of His displeasure. Her delay in reporting her husband's sins was not because of this accursed trip. It was because of her own selfish frailty.

Hot tears trembled in the corners of her eyes. She did not love her husband, nor did he care for her. Their marriage had been the usual kind, a joining of property and alliances. In the beginning, they had bedded regularly enough to produce several children. Her suitably wide hips had borne the promised healthy babes. Only two had died just after birth and a few more God had taken while they were still in her womb. But her husband's dutiful grunting as he rubbed himself inside her body always bored her. She never bothered to pretend there was any pleasure, nor had he. Only once had he spent the entire night in her bed. That was meant only for show on the wedding night and to display proof of her virginal bleeding the next morning. When he'd left on crusade, she was grateful. There would not be any more of that marital debt nonsense for a long time, and, she had realized with a hint of hope, many men never came home.

But she did care for her children. If she revealed that her husband had sinned against the English king, their children would suffer grievously. Her husband would likely be beheaded, or worse if King Edward willed it, and their own Scottish king was both brother-in-law and friend to him. King Alexander III might join in stripping their lands and income. Monarchs could always use land, either for them-selves or as gifts to friends. She would take vows, and her family would make sure she had funds for a comfortable retreat from the world, but her children might well starve, be imprisoned, or both. Few were foolish enough to defend or support the spawn of men who were traitors to the mighty.

As these thoughts faded, no comfort came to her soul. The only sound in the chapel was dripping water from ceiling leaks and the high gaping windows. The wind had grown strangely hushed. Despite her admission of fault and a plea for tolerance from God in the last few minutes, the menacing aura grew increasingly oppressive. Nor had she felt such dread before in a place dedicated to prayer.

"And that it still is despite the appalling failure to honor God with proper care and shining ornamentation," she murmured aloud. This complaint was uttered mostly to make sure she was still capable of breathing in the dense silence.

As her words faded into the frosty air, she heard a soft footstep behind her. Looking over her shoulder, she first gawked in disbelief and then gasped in terror.

Her shock destroyed all speech, but her soul screamed a silent protest against what her eyes insisted was real. She swiveled around on her knees to face her nightmare, lifted one hand and reached out in supplication.

The knife slid easily into her heart.

She did not even resist.

D avid, Earl of Ness, rose to his feet, brushed away a
few rushes caught on his robe, and smiled.

"Cousin, your gesture honors the Queen of
Heaven well, but it was not required for her most humble of
servants." Prioress Eleanor, head of Tyndal Priory, turned to
ask Sister Serena to bring refreshment, but the young nun
had disappeared.

"I wanted to show respect for you as well," he replied.
"My mother would have expected me to do no less. She not
only loved you like a mother, but she was proud of your
accomplishments in service to God."

Eleanor felt her face grow hot with embarrassment. The
earl's mother, Sister Beatrice, had retired to Amesbury
Priory after the death of her husband and their children had
reached an age to marry or take on adult responsibilities.
Despite her high rank, she refused any higher monastic
position than novice mistress, but when Eleanor's mother
died in childbirth, Sister Beatrice had asked permission
from Prioress Ida to bring her little niece there and raise her.
Approval had been instant, and Eleanor then found a loving

home with her aunt in the beauty of Amesbury, as well as her future vocation.

"Your mother was a very kind woman," she murmured. "I loved her with all my heart."

"But she was also one who neither suffered fools nor uttered lies," her cousin said. "She never gave compliments when they were unwarranted."

Eleanor turned away to avoid response and looked again for the absent nun, but she had still not materialized.

Gazing back at her cousin, she found the resemblance between Sister Beatrice and David very strong today. He had that same expression of mixed humor and compassion in his eyes. His smile was also an exact replica of his mother's. He had much charm, although it did not mean he was shallow or arrogant. Any man who assumed otherwise would quickly learn of his error.

She had always been fond of David, although he was much older than she. As a young lad of fifteen, he had been less than eager to tolerate the company of a small girl when he visited his mother at Amesbury. But he had dutifully obeyed his mother's order and eventually learned to enjoy talking with Eleanor as they both grew older and she more capable of adult conversation.

Now he rarely visited England, choosing to remain in his Scottish lands inherited from his father, but they sent each other family news, and the closeness had remained intact over the years. When he visited King Edward, as he was obliged to do for matters of war, acts of fealty for the English lands he held, or because the king simply enjoyed his company and sharing tales with another crusader, David tried to visit Tyndal Priory as well. For many years, he had done this without his wife, a woman who would find any excuse to avoid accompanying him. The last time Eleanor remembered seeing her was just before she left Amesbury to take on this leadership of Tyndal. Why Eda had inexplicably travelled with her husband on this current occasion remained a mystery.

"Has your wife already returned to Scotland?" Eleanor realized she had not even thought of the woman until now. Her memory of the countess was vaguely unpleasant. Eda had been attractive enough years ago, although her eyes had never been kind. As Eleanor recalled, the woman had not hidden her contempt for those she deemed beneath her but was forced to treat with courtesy. Her sour gaze lightened only when Sister Beatrice approached. Eda was quick enough of wit to realize the dowager countess might have retreated from the secular world to serve God, but she remained dangerous for any mortal to offend.

"She will join us here shortly. She begged permission to visit one of the small chapels first so she might honor God with grateful prayer for our safe journey so far." The twinkle in David's eyes had vanished.

Eleanor did not disparage anyone's desire to offer such prayers, but she sensed from her cousin's tone that his wife's piety displeased him. As for his own faith, he had taken the cross and actually gone to the Holy Land. That suggested a deeper than average devotion. Many of his rank, and even kings, had sworn to go but found cause never to do so. So why did he have this reaction to his wife's decision to visit the chapel before coming here to greet the priory leader?

"God will be pleased," she replied. "We shall delay our meal until she arrives." Indeed, Eleanor thought with growing irritation, the delay was welcome since Sister Serena had yet to appear even long enough to pour a mazer of wine or offer a pittance of cheese. Walking over to the place where the ewer of wine sat, she poured some and took the cup to her cousin. "What is the latest news from court?"

"Your eldest brother sends his love," he said after

9

sipping the drink with evident appreciation. "He is well and remains in the king's highest regard."

"Has our queen made any progress in forcing him to marry?" Eleanor grinned. Baron Hugh's resistance to these efforts was impressive, although she knew the reason was a sad one. The only woman he had loved was dead, and all hope that he might recover from this had been vanquished by the damage done to his soul during his crusading time in the Holy Land. He did have one son, albeit illegitimate, but had made it clear that their married middle brother, Robert, was responsible for producing any heirs to title and estates.

He shook his head. They shared a laugh, and David went on to other news.

"Did you know that the king and queen have decided to offer their daughter, Mary of Woodstock, to the Order of Fontevraud when she is older?"

Eleanor shook her head. That was the girl the queen had birthed when Eleanor had also been in Woodstock to say farewell to her dying father. Despite her grief, she had been required to capture a murderer while keeping the news of the crime from the suffering queen so she might not have more worries than whether she or the baby would live. Queen Eleanor had remained grateful ever since.

As her cousin continued with details, Eleanor grew more perplexed by his news. In principle, she did not agree with giving a child to God's service before the child was old enough to make such an austere life choice herself, and she had heard that the royal parents felt the same. Little Mary was surely only four or five years old. Eleanor wondered why this decision had been made and could only hope the girl found a vocation for the path she had not chosen.

"And have you heard about the execution of Dafydd ap Gruffydd, Prince of Wales?"

"No! Only that he, as well as his wife and several children, had been taken prisoner in June."

"Just before I arrived at court, he was dragged behind a horse to the execution ground, then hanged, drawn, and quartered by King Edward's command."

Eleanor gasped. "Traitor to his word he most certainly was! But he was of high rank and wed to an Englishwoman, also of fine lineage. Am I not right that this form of execution in the time of our current king's father was reserved for those of much lower standing? Why was he not beheaded? That execution was appropriate to his status."

David's face grew pale. "Away from the king's ears, several others asked the same question. Some claim that King Edward wanted him to suffer great agony because he had shown him much kindness and many favors, only to have the prince thank him with rebellion and broken oaths. Our king does not like being mocked when he extends the royal hand filled with favors. His father had been most generous with gifts and forgiveness and was often repaid with more disloyalty. King Edward will not be used or be the object of any man's contempt. I am grateful that I did not arrive earlier and thus have been required to witness the death. There is little cruelty I have not seen on the battlefield done to soldiers alive or to their corpses, but this is a death that exceeds all in brutality." Instinctively, he looked around to see if he had been overheard.

"And King Edward felt no remorse later?"

"Perhaps I am being unkind, but I think he reveled in it. He said that the terrible execution would stop others from committing treason or breaking their oaths to him."

Although she did not say it, Eleanor disagreed. If the reality of an eternity in Hell was not enough to stop men from sinning against God, why did a mere earthly king think far briefer punishments would keep others from committing crimes against him? King Edward, with his especial dedication to touring holy sites, should know this better than most. Nor did she think the precedent was a good one. Escalating the cruelty of execution only made men long to inflict even greater pain, or so it seemed. She would never understand why it gave so much pleasure to watch human agony but far less to act with compassion and forgiveness.

With a crash, the door to the audience chamber burst open and banged against the wall.

Both cousins leapt to their feet.

A young nun stumbled into the room and waved her arms. "My lady! You must come immediately!" She then saw the Earl of Ness and stared as if he were a monster emerging from the nearby stream. Jerking her gaze away to rid herself of this apparent apparition, she gasped: "Sister Anne says it is urgent!"

3

T he bells had just rung for the next Office.

Barring other sacred duties, all monastics were on their knees, chanting devotion to the God they served. Those in the priory with more worldly purposes, such as the sick waiting to be seen by the hospital attendants or the merchants bringing wares to sell, grew hushed out of respect for this time dedicated to worshipping the Deity they often feared and sometimes loved.

Brother Thomas had chosen to accompany Mistress Megge and her two sons back to their small but comfortable wooden wagon, attended by the armed guard that waited to take the family home to Norwich. The walk was done in a companionable silence. Both adults were deep in unshared thoughts, but each was equally aware that they both had reason to feel unease over the future and faced heart-breaking loss.

The earth remained frozen after the bitter night. Although the last snow had melted, except in the deepest shadows of the priory, Brother Thomas felt a brief unde-fined pleasure in the steady crunch of his feet on the brittle path. Glancing at the woman beside him, however, he saddened. Where might she find solace in the days or even, if God were kind, years to come? No matter how much she adored her little sons, she was still a woman young enough to long for the daily company of a good husband and the comforts found in the marriage bed.

Mistress Megge caught his glance and smiled.

There was neither mirth nor mockery in that. As Thomas had realized with his usual talent at observation, she was a kind woman who understood the world far better than most. Although he doubted she ever spoke of her perceptions and had learned that she faced the complexities of humanity in the light of faith, he suspected she never ignored danger or cruelty in men's souls. She might deal with the problems as diplomatically as possible, but she was prepared to become a she-wolf if necessary to protect her family. He was grateful that she seemed to have concluded he was not an evil creature.

"I think we shall both miss my husband, Brother. I for his sweet companionship, and you for the earnest seeker of justice he was before he suffered this terrible injury. We knew two different aspects of him, but that does not lessen the sense of loss we each feel."

Thomas felt a bite of grief. Durant was not dead, yet she spoke of him as if he were.

The former wine merchant's eldest son, the monk's godson and namesake, looked up at his mother with a worried frown. "Shall we not visit our father, then? You said we would."

She squeezed his hand. "Of course we will! Often and soon enough again. Now you and your brother must close your ears to the words exchanged between adults. They are far beyond the ken of children."

Even her admonition was warmed by her love for the boys, Thomas thought, then he saw the eldest look to him for further guidance. The world had already begun to teach the lad that a man's instruction took precedence over that of a woman, even a cherished mother. Thomas quickly nodded concurrence of Mistress Megge's instruction but asked himself what the boy would do without his father available to provide this need.

Once a man, the boy might learn, as Thomas had after years of serving Prioress Eleanor, that Eve and Adam had once shared the same body created by God. In separating from him, Eve had taken with her elements of wisdom just as she had one of his ribs. If he could, Thomas would help both boys understand that dismissing a woman's perceptions and advice was like ignoring the complexity of God's creation. He would talk to Durant about doing this. He suspected he and the wine merchant would agree, but Thomas did not live close enough to the boys to advise as often as needed. Teaching effectively would not be easy.

Mistress Megge stopped. They were close to the wagon taking them back to a house that would feel empty and silent without Durant. She looked down at her boys and sent them off to the waiting armed guards. They ran with eager anticipation to one man of whom they seemed fond. "Are all boys, even those destined to be merchants, so enamored with swords and spears?"

Thomas smiled. "I fear there is truth in that, mistress, although most of us soon find delight in other things. Your lads may well lose their joy in weapons of war as they grow older. At their ages, blood usually means a cut finger or scuffed knee. They do not see death in it."

She nodded before looking at him with the hint of more perception than her next words might suggest. "You chose to take vows and serve God."

Although he knew she would not ask probing questions

no matter what his reply, he decided a nod of agreement was sufficient.

Looking back at the quarters where Durant had chosen to spend whatever remaining days God had given him to live, she said, "My husband told me about the treasure he buried near the privy behind our house. I did not know about the service he had been rendering the king until he came home nearly dead of his wounds. It was then he fully explained how he met you and the bond of brotherhood you had each sworn to the other after facing death together." She shook her head.

Was that gesture meant to banish the memory of the circumstances of the revelation by her husband, Thomas wondered, or was it the pain she must have suffered when learning that her husband had long had a life quite secret from her? He would not be surprised that she would also be deeply hurt that Durant had revealed more of himself to a stranger than he had to his wife of many years.

"The wine business alone would have given us a comfortable life, Brother. This surprise gift means our boys can choose the paths they wish in life and that I shall have the dowry I need when the time comes for me to take vows."

Although this last admission should not have been a surprise, Thomas was at a loss for reply and let a respectful silence suffice as response.

"He did explain that his secret was meant to protect us," she said, "and that he had told you everything in case he never found the right moment to speak to me. I am glad he did, Brother. A wife may share many things with her husband, but she is still a woman. He had no brothers and his father was dead. He learned he could trust you, and you gave him that masculine bond he needed."

She reads thoughts so well, he thought with more admiration than unease. She had said all this with no hint of resentment, yet he still suspected she was deeply hurt that Durant couldn't sufficiently depend on her.

Suddenly, he looked at her expression with more care. Or did she know that he and her husband shared a love that demanded a union far more likely in a marriage bed than common to brotherly affection? Was that the cause for her sorrow and not that her husband lacked masculine support? He felt an icy shiver that had nothing to do with the winter chill.

A burst of childish laughter was a welcome distraction. The armed guard was holding his upright sword next to the youngest son. The hilt extended over the lad's head, much to the amusement of both boys. What speech they all shared was more evident from the white puffs of frozen breath than by any words overheard.

"He respected your skills and advice with gratitude and great love, mistress." Thomas wished he could ease the pain if she did suspect the nature of the love he and her husband had shared. "He often said that his business would not have been as successful if you were not the talented manager you were when he was absent. He..."

"You are kind, but please do not humor my frailty," she said. "I fear I have allowed myself to show my selfish and worldly sorrow at this parting with my husband." She raised her chin in defiance of her weakness. "At no time did I doubt his devotion to me or our boys. It is wicked of me to regret that he has decided to end his days in this priory and in..." She bit her lip.

For the first time, Thomas heard a hint of defensiveness, and then watched as she swallowed the emotion and turned to him without any suggestion of either jealousy or bitterness.

"Bring him to God, Brother," she said softly. "He needs you, and only you, to help him cleanse himself of sins.

17

Above all else, I want him to join the angels when he dies. As for my own soul, I will seek a path that will address my personal wickedness." With that, she hurried toward her boys and the journey back to Norwich.

Thomas hesitated before following. To his shame, he felt resentment and believed that she had the far easier time than he in dealing with her human frailties. She possessed Durant as any wife did. Their union was blessed by God and honored by good men. Durant himself loved her as his life companion. That their relationship was more that of brother and sister, other than the rare times they had bedded to produce children, was irrelevant. If God was pleased with their penances, the pair would meet again in Heaven and embrace with the chaste love they had actually preferred.

But Thomas could never hope for an equal reunion after death and was convinced he would never breathe the sweet air of Heaven. Durant's lust for him or any man might have been destroyed by the agony of his castration, near death, and the belief that this was his punishment for his sins, but Thomas was not relieved of desire nor of his constant demands for explanations from God. Of late, his dreams of coupling with faceless men had increased, as had his joy with the inevitable release until he fully awoke to a world and values that hated those acts and contentment. Indeed, he had begun to pray for a return of the impotence he had suffered for so many years after he had been repeatedly raped in prison.

Nonetheless, he would do his best to help Durant make peace with God because Brother John had ordered him to do so as his penance for what had happened on the border of Wales. And he would also do so because he cared for the wine merchant in so many other ways than that tormenting longing to couple together.

As he now hurried after Mistress Megge, he understood that they both had reason to be jealous of the other. She could never have that closeness her husband had shared with him. He could never enjoy the legitimacy of union that she owned with the man they both loved.

It was a situation Thomas regretted for them both. Any competition between them would never be resolved because neither one could ever win.

4

Prioress Eleanor would have arrived at the chapel far more quickly if Sister Serena hadn't concluded that she must literally lead her mistress there. Either the nun thought Eleanor was incapable of exceeding the pace of a snail or she was convinced Eleanor had forgotten the way —as she obviously had herself. She also provided a detailed commentary on how to return by the least expeditious path.

Trying to blunt her annoyance by praying to endure the incompetence of this child, Eleanor reminded herself at least a half-dozen times that she had been too spoiled with the attendance of her two former maids. Yet a stubbornly insistent voice in her head kept interrupting her orisons. Was this really the only young nun or lay sister who could be spared to serve as her attendant, or had God deliberately sent Sister Serena to force her to learn greater charity?

"We could walk a little faster," Eleanor suggested to the nun. "I am not yet of Methuselah's age."

When Sister Anne saw her prioress approach, she rose from the side of the corpse and hurried to her.

All it took was one glance for Eleanor to know who had died and to suspect the grave nature of that death. Immediately, she sent her attendant nemesis to stand with a couple of lay sisters some distance away. No matter how much the girl had provoked her, she had no wish for this child to see the cruel details of such an end to life.

Struggling to control her own shock, Eleanor clutched the sub-infirmarian's arm but kept her voice to a whisper. "My cousin's wife!"

"There is worse news," Sister Anne murmured. "I have no doubt that she was murdered."

Eleanor approached the body and carefully knelt beside it.

Sister Anne moved the small crowd of monastics some distance away so Eleanor could have a few moments to recover from her distress and gather the details she needed to assess the crime. The nun did, however, make an exception for a few in the group.

One was a particularly odiferous priest. The other was a wailing young woman who appeared to be a servant. A third was Prior Vincent, newly elected to the position after the death of the much-loved Prior Andrew. The sub-infirmarian noted that Vincent's face had taken on a greenish pallor. If the man was going to vomit, Sister Anne thought, she hoped he would do so outside. As a hint, she not so subtly gestured in the direction of the door.

He either ignored her or didn't see her hand. In either case, he remained where he was, gaping at the sprawled corpse and continuing to turn an ever more sickening hue.

The sub-infirmarian gave up and went to kneel beside her prioress. "A lay sister came for me," she said. "As soon as I saw how this woman had died, I prayed you would come quickly. She has not been dead for long. The body is still warm to the touch, although it is cooler than a living mortal. As of this moment, I know of no witnesses to the deed."

Eleanor reached out and touched the knife extending from of the chest of the dead woman. "Only to you dare I say this, but this knife belongs to my cousin. His mother gave it to him when he was knighted, and he cherished it. Yet he has been with me in my chambers for some time. The candle burning for light, which was lit as he knocked for entrance, had diminished an amount that is common for about an hour's span when I was summoned."

Sister Anne did not need to tell the prioress that death might well have occurred some time before that candle was lighted, taking into account the chill chapel air. Such details could be discussed later. "I will say nothing to anyone." She hesitated. "But what about Crowner Ralf? He must be summoned when he returns."

"I do not intend to keep any information from our crowner, painful though that might be," Eleanor said. She slowly pulled her hand back from the weapon, as if regretting that she must leave it visible, and then stretched it out to examine the ground around the body.

"I found no wounds on her hands to suggest she had tried to deflect the blow. Yet she must have seen her assailant. As you can observe, she fell backward and to one side. I believe she was kneeling when struck but was facing him." Sister Anne continued to keep her voice low. "The angle of the knife shows he struck from above her."

"Him?"

"A convenient term. It could have been a woman who killed her."

Eleanor lifted one of Eda's lifeless arms, pulled one shoulder up, and pointed out a light and delicately jeweled cross on a slender gold chain. "What is this?"

"I did not see that," the sub-infirmarian said.

A gagging noise interrupted their discussion. Eleanor looked up and saw Prior Vincent standing all too near and about to vomit on both corpse and the two kneeling women.

Eleanor jumped to her feet and edged him back by moving a bit too close to honor their mutual vows. "Tell me quickly. What do you know of this?" She needed to ask, but she also hoped to distract the man long enough to move him away before he spewed.

Swallowing noisily, he coughed out, "I found her. Sent a lay sister for you. Stayed to keep the curious away."

"Did you see or hear anything?"

He cautiously shook his head, but his expression showed that he was still able to display annoyance over the question despite his queasy stomach.

"Then go back to the men's quarters and question all the monks and lay brothers under your rule to see if anyone did. I shall summon you later for a report."

He hurried away, but not before glaring at his prioress and muttering, "Had wit enough to do it without your orders."

But you did not have wit enough to leave before you possibly destroyed evidence, dishonored a dead body, and certainly embarrassed yourself, Eleanor thought. If he was angry, so be it.

The sub-infirmarian stood and watched him flee. A moment later, she was almost certain she heard him throwing up in the grass outside the door. She didn't like the man and was convinced Prioress Eleanor shared her opinion, but she did feel some pity for him. Presumably, he had never been a soldier and had had no contact with murders. "The same lay sister also summoned me," she said quietly to her leader, "and she did so without direction from our new prior. who forgot the need for my observations."

Eleanor briefly smiled, then inclined her head toward the remaining couple who had not moved away. "Who are the two standing just there?"

"The weeping one claims to be the maid to the Countess of Ness. Her name is Jennet. The fellow next to her is the countess's priest, or so he says. Father Fithian." Sister Anne wrinkled her nose. "From his reek, I would say he might be better named Father Fetid."

With a sympathetic glance at her friend, Eleanor gestured for the couple to approach and tried to greet them with a comforting smile. "I would know your names since you are strangers here."

The priest lowered his head. When he spoke, he mumbled. "I have been the priest for the Countess of Ness for many years." He tilted his head toward the weeping woman beside him. "That is Jennet, her maid."

Eleanor hoped this priest gave directions for penance in a clearer voice, but her hearing was excellent, so she had no problem understanding his mutterings. She thanked him, then turned to the maid. "Were you with your mistress when she came in here?"

"Neither of us were," the priest replied.

Eleanor waited for more information from either of the two. The priest's head remained bowed, so she could not see his expression or if his lips moved at all. The maid was still wiping tears from her cheeks and gulping back sobs.

"Where were you if not by her side?"

The priest looked heavenward and blinked several times as if confused by this question. "Our lady told us to wait outside while she prayed."

"Did you see anyone enter the chapel or leave it soon after your mistress went inside?"

Father Fithian remained perplexed and then rubbed his nose as if that would clarify his confusion. "We are strangers here. Your religious are unknown to us. Why would we notice anyone, or if we did, how would we know their names?"

Irritated by his response and suspecting that the maid might not be allowed to speak unless she was alone, Eleanor decided any further questioning of the pair now was likely futile. "Then return to your separate quarters. After I learn more about the details of this crime, I will arrange to speak to you both again, separately and in private."

For the first time, the maid looked at her. A hint of fear briefly appeared in her eyes, then just as quickly vanished.

The priest frowned, but Eleanor sensed no anger in that. Perhaps, she decided, he was simply a man who suffered from frequent confusion.

"I must insist that you both stay in your separate quarters until you are summoned. Admit no one inside except the person I shall send." Eleanor gestured to Sister Serena. "She will be my messenger. Take good note of her face." Instantly, she regretted that decision. She would have to go herself or find another safe way to question each. The nun would not be a reliable messenger.

As the two left the chapel, Eleanor watched them. The priest did indeed suffer from a rank odor. Although some religious deemed cleanliness to be a luxury, a physical comfort, and most assuredly wicked, most of those preferred a hermetic life. It was an attitude she did not tolerate in her priory, and she wondered how her cousin's wife had endured it. As for the maid, she had gotten little sense of her other than the tears which seemed genuine. Her willingness to let the priest answer for her was not surprising. She was a maid and a sinful daughter of Eve. As such, her voice was deemed of little value. In this crime, however, Eleanor would demand that Jennet speak freely in the privacy of her audience chamber. Had God not

25

allowed Eve to tell her version of the apple-and-serpent tale?

She called to Sister Serena and told her to immediately find and bring Brother Thomas to her chambers, then she joined Sister Anne, who was talking to two lay brothers.

"I will need privacy to further examine the body beyond the immediately observable," the sub-infirmarian said to her. "With our crowner still in Norwich, and his exact return unknown, he will need any details we can provide while the corpse is still fresh."

"Do you anticipate finding any complications in the manner of death?"

"No, so my examination should not take me long but must be done. Unless there are marks on her body that are hidden by her clothes, the knife is the obvious means of killing her. You and I have observed the immediate area with care. You found that bit of jewellry and can confirm the location." She looked with sorrow at the corpse. "In all kindness, we cannot leave her body on the floor for all to see, and I need to strip the corpse."

"At least Ralf knows he can trust our observations, and he will need whatever you learn from your examination. I agree the body should be removed for your observations, then placed as soon as possible near the altar in one of our chapels for God's protection until her husband can decide on burial. Perhaps in the hospital? Take any room you need for your work. I will be in my chambers awaiting your findings." Quickly, she bent and picked up the cross bearing necklace. "I must take this to ask if anyone can identify it, but I should leave the knife in place." She shuddered. That seemed so cruel, but Eda was dead and could no longer feel the pain.

While the sub-infirmarian arranged for the transportation of the body, Eleanor turned and almost bumped into

Sister Serena, standing immediately behind her. "You have found Brother Thomas so quickly?"

The young nun wrung her hands. "I could not do so, my lady. I do not know where the good monk is and did not know if I would endanger my vows by going alone or if I needed an older nun to accompany me."

"He is most likely with Master Durant, the man who just arrived to take up permanent residence in our old guest quarters. As for proper attendance, take that lay sister over there with you. Her company should be adequate, and she will know where to go."

As Sister Serena stumbled off to collect the designated lay sister, Eleanor closed her eyes. They burned with the strain of too much unrelieved aggravation.

"The child means well, Lord, but she does try my soul," she whispered.

5

Durant lay in bed, his head and back supported by thick pillows. A cover had been tucked carefully around his shoulders. Although a splendid fire danced with crackling joy in the fireplace nearby, it struggled to blunt a cold so keen it felt capable of cutting a man's flesh.

Brother Thomas nodded to the lay brother who had been assigned to care for Durant and told him he could leave to attend the next Office. Then he forced himself to smile at the patient and hoped his worry and aching heart were well concealed.

The wine merchant, once strong, lay in wretched frailty. His eyes had sunken so deep into his skull that their color was no longer recognizable. His flesh was a blotched gray, and his cheeks were gaunt. If Thomas had not known that his beloved had walked the earth for no more than two score years, he would have sworn he was a man of great age and must be praying daily for death.

Durant managed to smile at the sight of him—or, as became evident, at the object Thomas held in his hand.

"Why have you brought a tree to welcome me to the priory?"

"Only one branch." Thomas thumped the long stick on the ground. He had carefully shaven off all rough bark and rubbed it clear of splinters. "This is the gift I hope will aid in your healing."

That brief levity seemed to have drained the wine merchant of all energy. He could not even shake his head. "It is too late. I fear I have come here only to die. It was selfish of me to cause so much trouble for all at Tyndal when I could have died at home with less disruption and fewer good people inconvenienced. What sins I own I will soon take to God and there beg His mercy."

Such words from the mouths of other men would have suggested self-pity. When Durant spoke them, they revealed a firm determination to take responsibility for his thoughtlessness as well as the graver sins of which he deemed himself guilty.

"Nonsense. You are not near death. You need sleep. You were fatigued enough after enduring a hard journey from Norwich. Then, on arrival, Sister Anne had her most skilled healers examine you in the hospital. After which, you were carried here, said farewell to your family, and I gave you little time to rest before coming myself. You are also feeling the effects of the mild dose of poppy juice our sub-infirmarian gave you."

"I mean no insult by this comparison to a woman, Brother, but you remind me of my mother. We men may discount a woman's strength and call her frail of wit and body, but I suspect we all secretly make an exception for our mothers. When one of her offspring was ill, mine showed the determination a hardened warrior would admire." He sighed. "Sadly, she saw all but me die. Now I shall as well, but I am grateful she is in Heaven and has God's arms to comfort her."

Resting the branch against the wall, Thomas approached the bed. "I have cause to be fierce about your healing, just as your mother did. Dare you deny me sufficient time to bring you closer to God, as you previously asked me to do?" Silently, he prayed Durant would listen and fight to live. "Choosing to give your soul so easily to Satan is the choice of an evil man, and I do not believe you are since you once longed for help to cleanse yourself of sin."

"I am an evil man, as you well know!" Durant briefly pointed to his crotch. "I do not willingly give my soul to the Devil, but I fully understand that I have little time to do adequate penance before death."

"Not according to Sister Anne. She has concluded that you might yet heal from your wounds, thanks to some foul salve she ordered a lay brother apply to the area around your groin. The treatment smells of rot, but she claims that makes it especially potent against many things that eat away at human flesh."

Durant frowned. "I would never doubt the wisdom of Sister Anne," he said, "but you know I have no strength left to fight."

Thomas forced a grin and pointed to the branch. "And thus it is my duty to help you regain your vigor, both physical and spiritual. With that bough, and my arm, you will learn to walk a little more every day—or every week. At first, you might only be able to sit on the side of this bed, but it is winter, and walking outside this building is unwise. Nonetheless, you must give yourself a goal for when the earth warms in spring. Perhaps you could choose to walk to the grove of fruit trees? The mill, I think, will be too far."

"The hives?" Durant's eyes twinkled briefly.

Thomas's heart filled with joy at the show of interest. He knew he was succeeding. "To sweeten your goal?"

"Do not make me laugh! Next, you will demand I eat."

"Indeed, I shall, but you know Sister Matilda's cooking. I have been told that she is preparing you special dishes to tempt you while obeying the instructions of our sub-infirmarian."

"If I give you my oath that I shall obey, will you kindly offer again to teach me how to live a more godly life? I never meant to sound ungrateful."

The love in Durant's look both broke Thomas's heart and warmed it. He took the man's hand and kissed it with the chaste love of a blood brother. "I swear it, but I must trouble you for one more effort before letting you sleep."

Durant nodded with a groan.

Thomas brought the branch over to the bed, pulled the cover down, and rolled Durant over so he could brace him into a sitting position while pulling his legs over the side. Looking at the merchant's naked body, he wanted to weep at the sight of how wasted it was, but he gritted his teeth and put the branch in Durant's hand. "Hold on," he said. "I will help you stand. That is all I expect you to try to do today."

Gritting his teeth, Durant clutched the branch.

Thomas began to lift him to his feet.

At that instant, the door to the room opened, and two women walked in.

At the sight of the wine merchant's naked buttocks, the older lay sister laughed, covered her mouth, and turned her back.

Sister Serena fell to the floor in a faint.

Thomas eased Durant back into the bed and covered him, then ran to kneel by the unconscious nun.

"She will recover." The lay sister grinned at the monk, then spoke to the wide-eyed Durant over her shoulder. "And

I apologize to you, good sir, for our rude entry. The door was slightly open. We did not think to knock."

"Are you sure she is well?" Thomas carefully examined the young nun's head for dents or lumps, then concluded with relief that she had not injured herself in the fall.

Nodding, the lay sister told the monk that Prioress Eleanor required his presence in her chambers immediately. Then, without saying more, she grabbed Sister Serena under her shoulders and easily dragged her out of the room.

As Thomas began to shut the door after them, he heard the lay sister say to the prostrate nun, "Enough of this silliness, lass. Sit up! All you saw was a vision of Adam in the Garden, and he most certainly did not think his nakedness was any cause for shame."

6

Prioress Eleanor need not have worried how to break the news to her cousin that a dead woman had been found in the chapel and it was Eda.

He interrupted her story with an expression so calm it was unnerving. "My wife, I assume."

"Did she suffer an illness that might lead to sudden death?" Eleanor had never heard that to be the case, but she wanted to announce Eda's death in a way that would elicit a response uninfluenced by the cause. No matter how close she and David were, murder made everyone a suspect in the beginning.

He shook his head.

"She was murdered, David." With no idea how to tell him the horrible news in a gentler fashion, Eleanor decided to be blunt. She was also perplexed by his initially casual reaction.

Her cousin sat back, reached for his goblet of wine and sipped. He refused to meet Eleanor's eyes. Instead, he stared at his goblet as if the workmanship was extraordinary. There was still no hint that he grieved or that he had yet to feel the full impact.

Eleanor knew the couple were not loving, but they had shared a life for many years, and Eda was the mother of his children. Did they hate each other so much that he simply did not care if or how she died? Or was he simply too deep in shock over the news? Yet he had immediately assumed that it was his wife who was dead, although he gave no reason for thinking that. Others might have been in one of many priory chapels. She had not been more specific when he made his odd comment.

"You must have cause to conclude that it was your wife."

He tilted his head and looked at her carefully, as if waiting to judge her reaction. "She was a woman who knew many secrets, Cousin. Perhaps she had finally learned one too many."

"If you feared she might come to harm, why not provide her with protection?"

His lips curved into a brittle smile, and his eyes narrowed. "She refused an earthly guard. She believed God would protect her because she was one of His favored ones."

"David, this is a murder. I must ask questions, as will the crowner when he returns."

"Of course."

"Who hated her enough to kill?"

"I have long known how much she enjoyed uncovering the transgressions of others. Despite her gender, she preened like a king's peacock with impressive joy. But I only recently discovered that she deemed it her duty to tell our local bishop of what she knew. He revealed many of these sinners in his sermons. Several lives were destroyed and some self-murders committed. Since this had been going on for years, and he claimed his source was God Himself, I doubt others knew she was the one instead. Of those who lived and tried to reconstruct their lives or those among the families of the dead, I saw none at the king's court, nor on

34

the journey from Scotland or afterward when we arrived at your priory."

"Why did she go to the chapel before greeting me with the expected courtesy? I am not finding fault. I am simply noting that her choice was uncommon, and she was killed there."

Shrugging, he said, "In truth, I know of no reason other than to pray, probably out of gratitude for our safe arrival, as I mentioned. She was known for the thick calluses on her knees." Suddenly remembering who the person was in front of him, he had the grace to apologize.

She was tempted to jest that she knelt on a pillow and thus her knees bore no such marks of piety, but she did not have the heart to even try. "Did she normally pray without an attendant? It is common to have a maid nearby. She even had her own priest here."

"She preferred solitude when she muttered away at God and did not want the ears of those she deemed less worthy than herself overhearing." He smiled. "Only on formal occasions such as Christmas or Easter did we pray together with the rest of the household multitude, but I accidentally did step into the chapel at home when she was there and heard mumbled speech from her. That was also how I learned of her fondness for discovering how others transgressed. I confess no shame in listening to her that day."

"You saw no suspicious stranger before she entered the chapel here? No one asked an odd question? There was no strange event that you might now recall, knowing she has been killed?"

He did not hesitate even a moment. "None."

"You have no idea why she was murdered here rather than at court or on the journey here?"

He shook his head.

Taking the necklace out of her pouch, she gave it to him. "Do you recognize this?"

For the first time, she saw a reaction. The slight quiver that traveled through his body was almost unnoticeable. Only his previously rigid silence and utter lack of emotion made the tremble so obvious.

He looked up as he fingered the piece, and she knew he longed to ask where she had found it. She remained silent.

"No," he said in a hoarse tone.

"Might it have belonged to your wife?"

"If it did, I never noted it. She was not one to adorn herself with simple jewels for ornamentation. But I confess that I rarely pay attention to a woman's dress or personal decoration."

"A servant? A wife of lesser rank than your wife?"

"A servant? I doubt it. The jewels are modest but not without value. As for other women, I repeat: I am more likely to note the hilt of a man's sword than any feminine bauble, with or without a cross attached."

Yet, she thought, you assessed the value of the jewels with only a swift glance which argues against a complete lack of familiarity with women's trinkets. She held out her hand and took back the object he was holding with that gaze of studied contempt.

"One last question from me, Cousin, although Crowner Ralf will surely have many more of greater merit for the solution of the crime." Hesitating in order to increase the tension ever so slightly, she asked, "Why was that knife your mother gave you to commemorate your knighthood used to kill your wife?"

David's mouth dropped open, his eyes bulged, and he jumped to his feet. The goblet of wine fell to the floor. "Impossible!"

That was at least a reaction, Eleanor thought, although

she wished it had not been the strongest one so far. "How so?"

He looked around frantically, as if he expected the weapon to appear out of thin air. "It was in my room. I left it there before I came here. It did not seem right to greet the prioress of a great convent with weapons of war." His voice dropped to normal pitch, although there was a hint of pleading in his last sentence. "Are you sure?"

"I have no doubt. Your mother was so proud of you and chose the design with great care. And I remember how you cherished the gift."

"Please, Cousin, let me confirm that it is missing. I do not mean to insult your memory or suggest you are in error..."

At that moment, Brother Thomas entered the room.

"Well timed, Brother," Eleanor said, then briefly summarized what had happened for the monk. "Please accompany my cousin to his quarters and help him search for the knife in question." She turned to the Earl of Ness. "I pray you find this weapon and prove my memory faulty. Let me know when you discover whether or not it is safe."

David looked at her with a mix of sorrow and anger in his eyes. "Do not play with me. I am not one of your witless suspects. I did not kill my wife. I had no cause to do so." Looking at Thomas, he merely nodded and turned to the door.

Eleanor took mercy on him. "Sweet Cousin, I do not believe you are guilty, but the crowner does not have the knowledge I do about your honor and goodness. If I did not send someone with you to search, he would have greater cause to doubt your innocence. This way, he can have no question that you told the truth about what you did or did not find."

"Then I apologize and thank you," David replied without turning around, but his tone had softened.

When the two men left, Eleanor knew there were questions she should have asked, but realizing her cousin would be a primary suspect had unsettled her. Speed in gathering the most basic details of this crime was most important now. She also needed time to make some crucial decisions, such as how to present any discovered facts to Ralf when he arrived.

Perhaps it was time to talk with Prior Vincent. She might have preferred putting that duty off for a while but that would have been self-indulgent. Looking around, she saw that Sister Serena had not returned with the monk, so she summoned a passing nun to bring Prior Vincent to her audience chamber.

7

Prior Vincent stood in front of his prioress with a sulky expression that might be found in a small child. In an adult, it was inexcusable. His impatience to be gone was made evident by his hands, which he clenched and unclenched with an annoying rhythm.

For more times than she could count, Eleanor knew she had betrayed her dislike of the man when he was in her company. When he became prior and she paid attention to him for the first time, she suspected he had once been handsome, a charm both genders often found appealing. His sharp objections to anything he deemed disrespectful suggested he may also have had worldly authority before he took vows. But his past had long meant nothing here. Before he was elected prior, he had been a monk like all the others. She had hoped to work with him as she had with Prior Andrew but quickly found him dull, easily offended, and generally exasperating. Her own manner toward him had become abrupt and chill.

"Please tell me what you know of the murder."

"I have nothing new to say." He sighed deeply as if

profoundly bored, disgusted by what he deemed a senseless question, or both.

That would be the polite conclusion. Instead, Eleanor knew full well that he resented her authority. His choice to enter Tyndal, which was led by a woman, suggested some priest may have chosen this as a severe penance, or else her new prior had been dismally ignorant of the rules of this Angevin Order. She suspected the latter.

"Tell me again." She matched his rudeness with impatience but regretted that. Revealing her irritability, an obvious weakness, gave him the edge in their ongoing struggle for supremacy in the relationship.

His snort was unmistakably contemptuous. "I entered the chapel. I saw the body. I found a lay sister. I ordered her to alert the sub-infirmarian and summon you. I assumed you wanted the nun called first so she would have time to examine the body and have something to tell you. I remained to keep the open-mouthed gapers away."

Eleanor ignored his lie about ordering Sister Anne to come. She knew the lay sister well enough to trust her version of the story. "And you had gone to the chapel because...?"

"I was looking for someone."

Eleanor waited for a name, then decided it was not worth the effort to drag it out of him unless absolutely required. "Did you see anyone else coming or going while you were there?"

"I do not waste time idly gazing around. When I have a purpose, I concentrate on it. I only noticed the corpse on the floor because I chose to stop briefly at the altar to honor God."

"I take that response to mean you did not notice anything else of note?"

"Did I not answer your question?"

Eleanor managed not to roll her eyes by firmly shutting them and then praying for patience. But the effort to raise her thoughts to a higher level failed. She deeply missed the competent Prior Andrew but had been ready to accept whomever was chosen by the monks. Her heart may have wanted the man to be Brother Thomas, but he had made it very clear that he was not interested and would refuse if picked over his clear objections. She had handled that disappointment too. What she was not prepared for was the choice of a man she found this difficult.

"Since we last spoke, have you discovered any monk or lay brother who was nearby?"

"These men have responsibilities to God. I cannot simply stop them in the midst of holy work for worldly matters. Yet I do not need to be told that the king's man will insist. I have taken time away from God to speak with each —and will complete that if I am allowed to return to my duties."

That means he has done nothing but may start soon, Eleanor concluded and bit her lip to keep from losing her temper. It took less and less to ignite her ire with him.

First among his many exasperating habits was his inability to utter Sister Anne's name. She was mentioned by title only or simply as "the nun". Did he really think his mouth would rot with corruption if he spoke a woman's name? Nor would he mention their crowner by name. This last omission directly disregarded the commandment ordering all men to render unto Caesar what was Caesar's. Did Prior Vincent believe that acknowledging the authority of an earthly king suggested the spiritual King had less? If true, that assumption was far more insulting to God.

Forcing herself to do so, she recognized that he had his virtues. He kept a steady eye on the morals and work habits of the monks and lay brothers under his rule. He had the sense to allow her to use Brother Thomas in her own service and never once questioned her about that. Nor did he treat her monk badly for his favored position with her. In fact, he utterly ignored him.

"Is that all, my lady? I shall report when I have something more to say."

She had to dismiss him after hesitating too long to ask more questions. Recalling all the ways he annoyed her every time she saw him was getting to be a bad habit. She had to break it.

But how had he escaped her notice for so many years? Most of the other monks had not. Why had her monks found him worthy to be elected their prior after Andrew's death? But now was not the time to delve further into that matter. The murder of her cousin's wife was of primary importance. Later, when she had some leisure, she might ask Sister Ruth.

She covered her eyes and groaned. That elder nun had just suffered from apoplexy, and Eleanor had been told that the woman might not survive. Yet she had failed to visit today, as she had sworn to do. Wincing, she begged God's forgiveness. Why was she failing so consistently of late in essential compassion and duty?

Hearing soft footsteps, she turned around and saw that Sister Serena had finally returned, albeit with a troubling pallor. She swallowed an unsympathetic comment and chose not to ask what had delayed her.

Why had God chosen this moment to give her so many opportunities to put her ever thinning compassion and patience on trial? She caught herself wishing the tests could be delayed until this murder was solved. After all, hadn't God chosen these crimes as her unique responsibility to resolve?

Suddenly, she wondered if she had simply been arrogant

in assuming God had done so. Wasn't Eda apparently convinced that God had also chosen her to reveal the sins of others? Yet Eleanor had found no personal merit in this odd duty, while Eda, according to David, had reveled in making many suffer when she made sure their secrets were made public. Nor did Eleanor seek out murder, while Eda dug like a ferret for hidden sin. The violence found her. Perhaps, Eleanor thought with sadness, God had decided she had little talent as a conventional nun and gave her this other, lesser work to compensate. "Enough of this," she growled at herself and looked at Sister Serena.

"Please bring me the maid of the dead woman. Her name is Jennet," she told the young nun. By the time she was through with this interrogation, Brother Thomas and David should have concluded that the knife of interest was indeed the one sitting in Eda's breast. Although she hoped they might find some bit of evidence to help in the solution of the crime, she knew she had probably already used up any credit with God after her recent wicked plea for reprieve from the trials presented by rude priors and incompetent nuns.

"My lady? I do not..."

"Take a lay sister with you. She will know where the maid is." If she was going to have to suffer the two aforementioned plagues, she decided to get some help with at least one of them.

Eleanor indicated that the time for further speech by the nun was over by turning her back and walking to her window. She did not look around until she heard the door safely close.

8

_____

Arthur, the great red tabby who was the terror of priory rodents but lovingly kept his prioress warm at night, approached the sobbing maid with caution, sniffed her shoes, and drew back. His mouth opened to reveal his sharp and gleaming teeth.

"A cat!" Jennet cried out in horror and leapt away.

"You do not like them?" Eleanor noted that her feline did not seem to fancy the maid either.

He yawned, turned his back on the woman, switched his tail up to expose his rear, and marched out of the audience chamber.

"They are Satan's creatures! I did not expect to see one in a priory..."

"Then perhaps their reputation for evil is unjustified. Cats are just one of God's many wondrous creations. It is thanks to Arthur and his many progeny that our food does not suffer from the attacks of an army of vermin." Eleanor had long been suspicious of those who disliked animals. She found the creatures miraculous in their variety and complexity, although she confessed there were a few exceptions to her admiration. Snakes and spiders were questionable, though she suspected God might not have a quarrel with her feelings about snakes.

It was obvious that Jennet was shocked to learn the beast even had a name, but she was wise enough not to pursue this. "I bow to your holy wisdom, my lady," she murmured.

Taking pity on the young woman, Eleanor gestured for her to take a seat on a nearby stool. Many of her rank would have required the maid to stand, but Eleanor knew Jennet had suffered a terrible shock with the death of her mistress. A little compassion was due.

"I have some questions for you, child."

"I know nothing! I do not even know how I shall eat now that my mistress is dead!"

"Surely your master will keep you on. He most certainly will not allow you to starve."

"But his next wife will bring her own maid, and his children have enough servants..."

Eleanor waved that aside. "Then he will find you a secure position but will not allow you to suffer in the meantime."

"Not just anything, my lady! I do not, for instance, deserve to be sent off to wash laundry. Not after being maid to the Countess of Ness!"

"Calm yourself," Eleanor said. "I shall speak on your behalf to my cousin. Now I need some information from you."

"I know nothing."

"Or perhaps you do but do not realize it." Before Jennet could reply, Eleanor continued. "How long had you served the countess?"

"I began not long after her husband returned from crusade. My mother was her former maid. When she died, the countess kindly took me on."

"You were quite young?"

"My courses had not yet begun. I have never known my age. But my mother trained me well in service to great ladies." Her chin rose with pride.

Eleanor smiled in acknowledgement of the young woman's assumed skills and shifted her queries back to the present. "What did you do when you arrived in our priory?"

"We were shown the guest quarters. My mistress required a separate room from her husband. Once her belongings were brought, I assisted her in changing her clothes. Her husband came to tell her that you had invited them both to your chambers. She told him that she must first find a quiet chapel where she could thank God for His many mercies. Only then would she come to greet you."

"How did she find the requested place of prayer?"

"Her husband asked someone. I do not know whom. I assume a lay sister or nun."

"Who took your mistress to the chapel?"

"Her husband. He took her inside a building where the chapel was. I did not see him leave, nor do I know where he went."

Eleanor was not happy to hear that. "I am confused. Did you accompany your mistress to pray or not?"

"I walked with her. Father Fithian had come with our master. The priest and I assumed we could also pray there in gratitude for our safe journey. Instead, my mistress stopped us before she entered the building with the earl and said we must remain outside. She wanted to pray in solitude. She said she would send for us if needed."

"Do you know how long her husband might have been in the chapel with her?" Eleanor knew this was an unnecessary question, but she hoped for any detail that would ease her fears about when her cousin had left.

"I cannot say. Perhaps Father Fithian noticed more than I."

"Did you see anyone enter or leave the chapel while your mistress was inside?"

"I walked about and did not stay very close to the building, my lady. It was cold, and I had to walk lest I turn into a pillar of ice. I kept my head down and saw little except the ground under my feet. As for Father Fithian, he is not inclined to companionable speech so he did not come with me. But he might have seen something unless he was deep in prayer as is his wont. I believe he remained near the entry for most of the time in case our mistress called on us to attend her, but I cannot be certain."

"How did you learn of the crime?" Eleanor decided that Brother Thomas should talk to the priest, but she would gather what she could from Jennet now so the stories could be compared.

"A lay sister. She only said that our mistress had died and she was on her way to summon you. We wanted to be by our lady's side, but the lay sister refused our request. We might stay nearby, however, but not go into the chapel until you or the woman from the hospital arrived and gave permission."

"Did you see the lay sister or Prior Vincent enter the chapel?"

"I saw no one. Perhaps the lay sister and your prior were already in the chapel? Please ask Father Fithian these questions." She stifled back a fresh sob.

They might have been in that chapel, Eleanor thought, but it was a little unlikely since the lay sister said she was some distance away when she heard Prior Vincent calling for help, and the prior commented that he had found the corpse not long after he had entered. There were other ways into the building where the chapel was, but the place was small and meant for private prayer. In the winter, most monastics preferred to remain in the Chapter House with its fire and pray at the assigned hours when there was the warmth from other bodies.

Eleanor realized she would have to ask Sister Anne to question all the nuns and lay sisters for her. The sub-infirmarian's skills were better used at the hospital, but Eleanor needed a reliable woman to query the female religious. She winced. If she had only taken the time to appoint a sub-prioress, a task long overdue, she could have assigned that woman to interrogate the female religious and keep Sister Anne at the hospital.

"Do you know of anyone who deeply hated your mistress, especially one who came here with your party from Scotland?"

Almost too quickly, the maid shook her head. "My mistress was a godly woman and known for her piety. How could anyone do aught but honor such a person? As a mistress, she was kinder than most. She never struck me, although I am sure I must have merited it."

"She never argued with anyone?"

The woman flushed, then shook her head again but said nothing.

That blush likely means Eda and her husband fought on occasion, Eleanor concluded with dismay. But details of marital quarreling was a subject that very few servants would dare answer honestly. "One final question," she said as she pulled out the necklace. "Do you recognize this?"

Jennet's eyes widened. Her ruddy flush paled to the color of snow. "I do not, my lady."

Eleanor held it out to the maid. "Please look more closely. It would belong to a woman, would it not?"

Taking the proffered item with extreme caution, as if she feared she might drop it, Jennet stared at the object without blinking. "I would agree. It is quite delicate."

"Might your mistress have owned it?"

"I cannot say with certainty, my lady. She did not wear much jewelry, only crosses, which she believed must be ornate to honor God. She believed decorating the body alone was something more worldly women did."

Taking the necklace back, Eleanor caught herself wondering which was the more worldly: an ornate cross, heavy in gems, or this one that was jeweled but modest in size and less conspicuous. She quickly dismissed the thought, hoping God would forgive her for any irreverence.

"Might it have been a gift from someone at court or from her husband? Would you know if she had gotten any gifts of note recently? Perhaps she mentioned something, but you did not see the item?"

"She did not usually speak of such gifts to me. If she chose not to wear such a thing, I might not be aware of it. I dressed her, but only at her direction. I recall just the crosses I mentioned. I was not familiar with any other jewels."

So the necklace remains a mystery, Eleanor thought, although she thought it odd that Eda was so protective of her ornaments that this item would never have been seen by Jennet. Neither the maid nor her cousin claimed to have seen it, yet she was sure both were lying.

"Very well," the prioress said. "Our crowner will have more questions when he arrives, but I shall let him know what you have told me."

Jennet's expression was akin to a sigh of relief.

And I have noted that as well, my child, Eleanor thought. It was odd that the anticipation of questioning by a king's man stirred less fear than one by a prioress. "In the meantime, I must go to your mistress's chamber to search for any hints of what might have been the cause of her murder. That will be useful to our crowner." She gestured to the maid to follow her. "Please accompany me. I need you to tell me what might be missing or moved after you and the Countess of Ness left for the chapel."

_____

9

"Shall I help you search?" Jennet stood next to Eleanor as she looked around the austere room.

"I will need you by my side to tell me if what I find or am examining is unusual in any way." Eleanor did not want the maid working on her own since she could hide or even destroy evidence out of guilt, a need to protect someone else who might have killed Eda, or out of loyalty to her dead mistress's privacy.

Jennet frowned briefly in what might be disappointment but then promptly agreed to help as requested.

The room was simply furnished, as any guest room in a priory would be. The bed was small but raised and designed to discourage any nocturnal rodents seeking a warmer nest or food. At the foot was a plain wooden chest for clothes and other personal items. A nearby table was placed against a wall with a basin of water on top for washing and a reddish pottery chamber pot underneath. In the middle of the floor, a table and bench for private meals held a small jug for wine and a couple of mazers. Further away and near the shuttered window, was the maid's bed, a straw pallet with a thin blanket. It was distanced enough from Eda's bed that the mistress would not step on her servant when she got out of bed at night. There were a couple of cresset lamps resting in shallow wall niches, ready to be lit when more light was required as the sun dimmed.

What did strike Eleanor as unusual was the addition of a raised writing desk on a small table near the window. Few wrote, especially women, and even those able to do so usually dictated to a cleric. King Edward used a cleric, but it was rumored that his mother occasionally wrote to her son in her own hand when she had especially personal advice to offer.

"Could your mistress write?"

"She did, my lady, although she usually had Father Fithian do so if the matters were related to running the household in Scotland or elsewhere under her care. She was unskilled in Latin and also wanted precision in her instructions."

Eleanor walked over to examine the desk more carefully. The table had nothing on it that immediately suggested anything related to the crime committed. A few fragments of parchment, scraped many times until the skin was almost too thin to reuse, were scattered around. But Eleanor carefully examined each bit to make sure she missed nothing significant. As she did, she noticed something light-colored buried deep in the rushes near the window. She bent to dig it out. It was another piece of parchment, but this one was thicker and had writing on it.

From the corner of her eye, she saw Jennet start. Eleanor assumed the maid could not read, but she also knew that such assumptions could prove wrong. After all, she herself was not only capable of reading and writing, she was fluent in Latin. She handed the parchment to the maid. "Is this your mistress's hand?"

"I cannot say for certain, my lady, but I believe it is."

"And that second word?"

Jennet shrugged. "It is just twists and swirls to me, although it most certainly is a very pretty thing."

Eleanor did not think Eda had had a fine hand. In fact, there were blots of ink and, to her mind, the letters were crudely rendered. But she took the parchment back and stared at it as if she were as confused as the maid by the writing. A quick scan established that the letter was addressed to a bishop near the Ness lands in Scotland and was unfinished. What she did note of potential interest was that Eda seemed to have learned something important during her trip to the English court. But the countess had stopped in mid-sentence, and there was no clue what this matter was.

Eleanor sighed dramatically and put the object on the desk. It could be left for Ralf to find since she already knew the story of Eda and her favored bishop. Next she moved on to the straw pallet and knelt.

"That is where I sleep, my lady!"

Even had she been inclined to ignore the pallet, the slight edge of fear in the maid's voice was enough for Eleanor to pay more attention and feel around the bed.

The straw was clean, as she expected it would be since no one had yet slept on it, but she saw a glimmer near the edge and reached into the straw for it. "What a lovely brooch," she said, holding it up to the light. The item was small but finely crafted. The gold was of good quality, the gems small but even in color.

"My lady's brooch!" Jennet extended her hand as if to snatch it away, then drew back. "She lost it after she arrived. We couldn't find it. Now she's dead..." She hiccuped a couple of times, but the effort was too labored to sound like a deeply felt sob.

"And beyond caring about such worldly things," Eleanor

said as she closed her hand around the item. "I shall put it back in her jewel case when I find it." Not for one instant did she think the object had been lost. The room was small. The light was strong enough to make the gems glitter. If she could see it, so could Eda and her maid. And, she thought with brittle humor, Jennet's instant recognition of the brooch tainted her argument that she hadn't any idea what might be in her mistress's jewelry collection.

Standing, Eleanor went over to the chest and opened it. The scent of fresh lavender was strong. Sprigs of the herb had been carefully placed throughout to repel fleas, possibly moths, and evil sprits. The clothes were made of finely spun wool, but the designs were simple and the colors dark. Only one robe owned a few flashes of color and a rimming of warm red fox fur. This, Eleanor concluded, must have been what Eda had worn when she was obliged to see the king and queen. A countess obsessed with her faith might choose a grim simplicity in what the English considered the wilds of the barbaric land to the north, but elegance of attire was demanded of her rank when she came with a husband doing homage to his English liege lord.

The box she was looking for had been carefully placed in the middle of the clothing.

When she opened it, Eleanor found nothing of great interest. A few golden rings of decent workmanship but owning neither gems nor elegance. There were three large and multi-jeweled crosses which matched in ostentation the one the corpse was wearing. What was most important was the fact the Countess of Ness owned nothing that even vaguely resembled the brooch found under the maid's straw pallet.

"Was this all your mistress's jewelry? Or did she leave much behind when she came south?"

"Oh, it was all, my lady! She did not trust some of the

lesser servants at home not to pass smaller items to one of their shaggy kinsmen while she was gone."

Eleanor nodded with a smile, yet this reaction had little to do with the rude remark about Scots with stealthy fingers. Where had that brooch come from? Surely Jennet was wise enough not to steal from her mistress, and the unusual plainness of the jewelry, other than the crosses, for this high-ranking woman suggested she had not. Yet it was obvious that Jennet had much to hide, including her knowledge of Eda's jewelry. Had the countess seen the brooch? Had she spoken to her maid about it? If so, it must have been just before Eda's death if the brooch hadn't been moved.

"Do you see anything out of place?" Eleanor looked around but saw nothing worth examining further. Her question was almost perfunctory. Now she was convinced that the maid probably wouldn't tell the truth if there were anything missing.

"Nothing, my lady."

The pair left the room. The brooch, however, was never put into the jewel box. Eleanor decided to slip it into her sleeve and ask her cousin if he might recognize this item, although he claimed not to care how women adorned themselves. If that were true, she thought, he has changed much in the last several years. He had always been a man with an easy charm around women as well as one who knew how to give compliments about what a woman needed most to hear.

10

_____

As she hurried back to her chambers, Eleanor was so deep in thought that she almost did not hear the voice calling out behind her.

Turning around, she smiled with delight.

Brother Thomas joined her. "I will not delay you for long," he said. "I just left your cousin after he had searched his room. When we arrived, he refused any offer of help, and I went to stand by the door to keep out of his way. Your cousin did not bring much on this visit. Except for two cloaks on pegs and his sword, all else fit in the trunk by his bed. I watched him go through that, and from what I could see, the items were neatly stored so I believe it unlikely that anyone else had searched his belongings. Of course he found no knife, and he told me that nothing else was missing. The knife, he said, had been placed next to his sword. He told me that he did not think the sword had even been touched. From his expression, I believe he was being honest with me."

"And what were his reactions as he looked but did not find the knife?"

"Angry at first, then he calmed." He hesitated.

"I want your honest observations and conclusions. He may be my cousin, but his knife is the murder weapon. I am not blinded by our kinship. He is a suspect." Eleanor knew her voice had trembled on that last sentence, but Brother Thomas would not fault her for it.

"His reaction was that of a man who had nothing to hide. He was angry at the theft, then he grieved over the loss of a much-prized possession. I am not sure he is fully aware that he is now a suspect. He was most upset about the loss of his dead mother's gift."

But he still has shown no sorrow over his wife's brutal death, she thought. Nonetheless, she felt some relief after hearing her monk's assessment. Anger over the use of his cherished knife to commit a murder was at least one normal reaction.

"I did not interrogate him, my lady. Ralf will do that soon enough. Had I made him fully aware that he was a suspect by posing questions, I feared his responses might well be tinged more with anger than any desire to assist in catching the killer. And like most, including the innocent, he would have more time to decide how best to protect himself from the crowner."

"As always, Brother, you are wise. Tell me all he said while you were there."

"He was silent during our walk to his quarters. When he could not find the knife, he told me that there was much time when the room was unoccupied. When you sent word that he and his wife were invited to dine with you, he went first to his wife's quarters to tell her. She, as well as her maid and priest, were there when he arrived, and all of them went together to the chapel. He did not think any of them could have slipped back to steal it, and he had no idea who else could have taken it. Since he knew he would have no need of him for some time, he freed his personal servant to find

57

amusement or rest. Without my asking, he added that he saw no one nearby, no one he recognized on his way to your chambers, and has no idea why anyone here would have killed his wife and especially with his knife."

"His man is trustworthy? Any other servants?" She was almost certain that his personal servant had been with him for many years and was loyal, but she needed confirmation.

"Yes, he is. He went on crusade with your cousin and protected him in battle. All others were sent to eat with the armed men in his company."

The obvious questions had been answered, but Eleanor knew her cousin was wrong about one thing. Either Jennet or Father Fithian could have run back to David's room after he left the chapel building for her chambers and even covered the short absence with a confessed need to relieve the bowels. Such a common excuse would be easily forgotten by the other. It might be unlikely that this happened but not impossible. "And his tone or demeanor?"

"By then his anger had vanished. He even apologized for his rudeness to me, which he said was most certainly undeserved. I saw sorrow on his face, my lady, and I do not think it was just the loss of the knife. He seemed troubled. Was he deeply grieved by his wife's death?"

"No, Brother, he was not. Other than the children she bore him, they had nothing in common. They never gained that comfortable or even loving companionship that some couples do over time who marry solely to increase family wealth or alliances." Eleanor opted to add more detail. "For years, his wife did not accompany him to our king's court. Why she did so this time was not mentioned by my cousin. He rarely spoke of her on those times he came to visit after his duty to King Edward was done." She looked the monk in the eyes. "I never felt he hated her. At worst, he disliked her, but that is not grounds for killing. They simply led different lives: he as crusader and military advisor to King Edward with the Welsh; she turned more to the Church."

"Yet they were long bonded. Might he have recovered from the initial shock of the news of her murder and begun to feel the sorrow anyone would feel for a spouse of many years? Even if they were not fond of each other, they had children together and many shared memories."

"That was what I expected, Brother, and was uneasy when I saw no indication of that when I told him of her violent death."

"My lady, had I been your cousin, I might well have reacted as he did. It is one thing to learn your wife, unloved as she might have been, has been murdered. It is another to hear that the killing was done with your own knife. The full implications of this may have taken time to occur to him, but he would have eventually realized that you were not the only one who will suspect him of the crime. If he has no idea why anyone would want that to happen, he might well feel fear. With courage, a man can defend himself against an enemy in the daylight, but it is hard to know what to do when the enemy is hidden in darkness."

She thanked him for that insight. "Sister Anne will report as soon as she has completed her more thorough examination of the body. It should not take long. Will you wait with me for her?"

"I had hoped to return to Master Durant for a brief while. Sister Anne said I should help him gain strength. She is confident that her current medications will ease his wounds better than those tried in Norwich, although she is unsure whether they will cure him. He is so weak that any increased strength will help his chances to survive."

As had been the case with the grievous thigh wound Prior Andrew suffered so many years ago while fighting for Simon de Montfort, she thought. The care from Tyndal hospital had given the good man many more years of life, but the wound had finally killed him. Tears stung her eyes. She swallowed them and winced at their bitter taste.

"I was just starting to get him out of bed for a few steps when Sister Serena... "

"Fainted at the door?" Eleanor tried not to smile. In her case, there was little of the world she had not seen or did not know. Her aunt had never believed that an ignorant mind was the same as a pure one and made sure her niece was especially comfortable with the distinctions between bull and cow. In Sister Serena's case, however, there was apparently a very great deal about God's earthly creatures the young woman had never known. With all the other tasks lining up like suppliants for her, Eleanor now added the need to teach the nun a few facts of life that any farmer's child would know.

"Go back to him," she said to her monk. "Come to my chambers when you are done, and either Sister Anne will still be there to inform you of anything significant or I shall."

He bowed and hurried off.

Eleanor watched him for a moment and realized she had forgotten to tell him that she wanted him to question Father Fithian. But she could do so soon enough.

As she started back along the path to her chambers, she noted that Brother Thomas had begun to change in positive ways of late. Brother John had been right to assign to him the penance of caring for Master Durant. Whatever evil we are tempted by, she thought, can often be vanquished by compassion and charity. The founder of her Order was known for facing temptation this way. And hadn't St. Paul said that of faith, hope, and charity, the greatest of all was charity? She had suffered from lust too, but God demanded she set all aside to serve His justice. Brother Thomas seemed to have rediscovered some joy in caring for the former wine merchant. What a confused thing love is, she mused.

But then she saw Sister Serena running toward her, and she sighed. That required charity had just fled from her heart.

"My lady! My lady!"

Eleanor wanted to grab her by the shoulders to stop her frenetic behavior. Why must she shout and wave her hands so? "Be quiet, child," she said as calmly as possible. "What is wrong? Take a deep breath and speak slowly."

"Nothing." The nun gulped for air. "You were gone so long. I feared someone might need you."

"But no one came asking."

"No, but what would I have told anyone if they had?"

"That you would send for me." Eleanor felt a sharp pain over one eye and prayed she was not about to suffer one of her terrible headaches. At least she had a packet of feverfew in her chambers that eased the pain. "But I will be in my rooms soon. In the meantime, you must go to Sister Anne and tell her that I will wait there for her report."

"I do not know where..."

"Take a lay sister with you. Most know how to find our sub-infirmarian."

And this task would give her a little respite from Sister Serena if a headache was coming.

There were so many things she needed to do. Too many. She must appoint a sub-prioress. With the death of Prior Andrew, she was having to grow accustomed to a new and annoying prior, which took up much time. Now Sister Ruth had suffered apoplexy, although she had been in increasingly poor health even before that. The two women had never been fond of each other after twenty-year-old Eleanor supplanted the older nun as head of Tyndal on the orders of

King Henry III, yet they had both, over time, learned mutual respect. Not to visit the nun's sickbed was inexcusable.

But when was she to find time to do anything with a murder to deal with? What clues did she have? What might they mean? What was the maid hiding? Or even the priest? Was her cousin hiding something? The crime might well become the sole problem of Crowner Ralf, but she was troubled by the additional question of why the crime had been committed in a chapel at Tyndal Priory. And she felt the increasingly heavy burden of knowing that her cousin was a suspect.

The dull winter sunlight burned through her eyes and into her head with sharp insistence. She winced, and her stomach roiled. This headache was promising to be one of her worst. It did not help that she wanted to believe her cousin was innocent but knew that he was either lying or deliberately omitting details that might prove important. This was one of the rare times she truly resented God's demand that she serve His justice.

Once in her private chamber, Eleanor could not bear to even glance at the accounting rolls she had set aside for immediate review. Even in the winter sunlight, the very sight of them seared her eyes. Instead, she took the feverfew remedy and closed the window shutters to dim the light. Feeling off balance and sick to her stomach, she lay on her bed and shut her eyes to banish the agony of any remaining light.

The cat jumped up so gently she hardly felt him, then he snuggled against her side. She rested a hand on his soft fur and was comforted.

As soon as possible, she would attack those accounts. Even if she had a sub-prioress, she would still take responsibility for most of the reviews. Her duties as prioress required that she guarantee enough income to properly feed and house her religious. That her leadership, the knowledgeable advice of Prior Andrew, and gifts from a grateful queen had provided more than a sufficiency of income was reassuring, but careful management was still demanded if financial security were to continue. Nonetheless, the loss of her beloved prior and the election of a man she deemed inadequate for the demands of his new position now required far more time on her part to make sure no errors were made and anything questionable was immediately resolved. And whom could she trust to travel to farms or rent-producing land and make sure all was run honestly and well?

Another surge of queasiness and pain made her whimper in spite of herself, and she swallowed to fight back the nausea. If God and Sister Anne's remedy were kind, she would look at the rolls tomorrow.

Her mind also longed to go back to the known details surrounding the death of her cousin's wife and think of those questions required to bring forth information needed to fill the holes in their knowledge of what had happened. But her headache throbbed, stabbed, and chased away all hope of even that minimal contemplation. The only thought she was able to retain was that she loved her cousin and did not believe he was a murderer. But she was increasingly convinced that he was not telling the whole truth. He might fool others, even the clever Crowner Ralf, but she had known David far too many years not to know when he was being evasive.

A loud banging on her door caused Eleanor to sit up and Arthur to flee to a far corner of the room. Swallowing stomach bile, she held her head and wanted to cry but forced herself to grant entry. No matter what awaited her, she could not stand for any repeat of that torturous sound.

Sister Serena threw open the door. "I brought you a goblet of wine, my lady! I had hoped..." Suddenly, she tripped and fell to the floor. The wine splashed across the rushes but not before bathing the nun's clothes in enough vintage to perfume her for days.

Eleanor's first thought was that there would be many drunken mice that night if Arthur chose to sleep elsewhere. Then she felt guilty and asked, "Are you hurt?"

Sister Serena wailed. "No! But I have spilled the wine, and I thought it would help you feel better!"

"Hush, child," Eleanor said, holding her head against the assault of the high-pitched lament. "The rushes will be changed tomorrow, and wine will not hurt the floor. It was a kind gesture to bring me the cup..."

"I will bring you another!"

"That is unnecessary." And indeed unwanted. When she suffered a headache, the last thing she wanted was wine, ale, or sustenance of any kind. The very smell of the wine was making her stomach churn, and she began to sweat. "If you will, open the shutters, child, and let the light in." She might not want the light, but the chill air might calm her stomach.

Sister Serena stumbled across the floor and jerked open the shutters.

Having closed her eyes against the sudden brightness, Eleanor felt the cold, took a couple of deep breaths, and her stomach calmed.

"Sister Anne sent word that she would come soon. I almost forgot to tell you."

Could anyone else be so careless, awkward, or incompetent? And why had she been chosen for this trial of having her as an attendant? But she knew who was to blame. If she had not been so reluctant to appoint a sub-prioress, there would have been someone fully able to review any candidates for entrance to the Order and to discuss all novices with the novice mistress. Instead, Eleanor had simply taken the word of the latter, a woman who was kind and dutiful but perhaps too disinclined to speak ill of any girl. As Eleanor recalled, the verdict on Sister Serena after her training was that she was "good". Sister Ruth, before she resigned as sub-prioress, would have added "and a trial to anyone having to deal with her".

"Sister, why did you choose to take vows?" It was a question Eleanor knew should have been asked when the young woman came to Tyndal for admission. But, again, she had assigned that duty to the novice mistress, who would be responsible for teaching them. A logical choice in many ways, but not, as it now seemed, the best. Eleanor had only asked the mistress if they were suitable, what dowry they brought, and if their desire to join this Order was acceptable. Serena had been found to satisfy all categories. Now Eleanor wondered if she really did.

The nun bowed her head.

Eleanor was not sure if the girl trembled or if her suffering eyes imagined it.

"I longed to leave the world, my lady." Her voice was barely audible. "Is it not a frightening, hateful, and wicked place?"

Eleanor waited, but Sister Serena failed to mention the usual reason given, that her faith demanded she spend her days praying in the confines of a religious house.

The nun continued to stare in silence at the damp rushes.

"Faith? A longing to serve God with prayer?" Eleanor knew she was hinting too strongly, but she was also curious about the response.

Sister Serena jerked upright as if prodded with something sharp. "Of course, my lady!"

Before any further word could be spoken, Sister Anne appeared in the doorway. Seeing her prioress sitting on the edge of her bed, the sub-infirmarian immediately assumed the cause. "Do you have enough feverfew?" The question was asked in a soft, low voice. "A little poppy juice might be helpful." She sniffed and tilted her head as she looked at the young nun, then at Eleanor.

"A little accident," Eleanor replied, knowing that she and Sister Anne would have laughed over the details had she not been suffering this headache. But now a wave of shame overcame her. It would have been cruel of them to do so. She looked at Sister Serena with sympathy and told her to leave the room but stay outside until summoned.

Sister Anne carefully closed the door behind the nun.

Eleanor sighed. "She is awkward, infuriating, utterly without talents, and yet she is kind. She meant to bring me a goblet of wine as a thoughtful gesture and spilled it all over the floor when she tripped."

Sister Anne nodded as she walked to the open shutters. "Is it better to have the air dispelling the odor or the light dimmed?"

"The spilled wine no longer matters. Please banish the light." Eleanor knew she was whining, not something she felt acceptable for a prioress, but the sub-infirmarian was her friend.

As Sister Anne dealt with the shutters, Arthur made his way back to his mistress's bed by avoiding the soaked rushes and pressing close to the walls. His nose twitched with displeasure. Carefully measuring the distance for his jump, he flew up on the bed without troubling Eleanor and once again pressed against her to soothe with his low purrs.

Eleanor petted him and realized that her headache was beginning to ease. "What more do you have to tell me?"

"Little enough, but I now have more questions," the sub-infirmarian said and copied the feline by carefully sitting near Eleanor.

12
_____

Durant leaned back against the chair and gulped air. His face was pale as chalk, and his body shook despite the wool cloak draped over his body.

Thomas knelt and held his hand. Had he demanded too much? Was Sister Anne wrong about Durant's ability to regain any strength? She was rarely in error. She usually knew when a condition was beyond her worldly skills and better left to acceptance and prayers. Yet the sub-infirmarian was still human and, by definition, flawed, the monk thought. She might have been mistaken this once. Thomas quickly begged God to forgive him if he had trusted a mere mortal too much and caused Durant to suffer more than he should.

"Thank you." Durant took a deep breath and squeezed Thomas's hand. "You give me courage."

"Was the walk too hard?" Thomas visually measured the distance from the bed to this chair.

"Please give me credit for my shuffles, Brother. I know it would have taken a healthy man three steps, but am I not allowed more?"

Thomas raised the hand he held, pressed it against his cheek, but did not reply. He was so grateful that the prioress had not only sent one of her own chairs immediately at his request. but had also provided an embroidered cushion to fit over the leather seat to soften it. Without asking, she understood that a stool would have been too low for a man as weak as the wine merchant, but this folding chair had arms, a slat in the back for support, and was the perfect height.

"You might be too kind to mention it, but I recall having to stop twice." Durant's breathing had calmed, although it still sounded a bit labored.

Thomas smiled. "A lesser man would have given up before he started."

"And I would chance losing my standing in your eyes by doing that?"

"My heart is not so easily lost."

Durant did not have the energy to continue the jesting. "But I have another worry. Did the two nuns see my grievous wound?"

Thomas shook his head. "Only your naked buttocks," he said. "I know the lay sister well. She is older and was once married. She politely turned her back when she entered the room and saw you. Her smile was proof enough that she witnessed nothing else. But Sister Serena has apparently never seen a naked man. She fainted, but after relaying the message sent by Prioress Eleanor, the lay sister assured me the young woman would be fine." He chuckled. "Then she literally dragged the girl out of the room. By the time I left, Sister Serena was sitting up on the floor, and the lay sister was urging her to stand up and stop fussing when no sin had occurred."

"Has the girl no brothers? Has she never seen boys swimming? We do not live in a world with space for privacy,

Brother. Men piss against walls in city streets and women lift clothes to defecate in fields. If her family was wealthy enough, her parents could at least couple without the children in bed with them. In any case, it is hard for anyone, and from a young age, not to have seen a man or woman unclothed."

Even in his father's castle, a man richer than the king, Thomas had come across men and women swyving remote corners. Once, he had seen two men and, quickly hiding, had watched in fascination. He had been old enough to feel guilty about his body's reaction but oddly happy to have seen them. Swallowing hard, he replied, "I know nothing about her past or her family background. She must have had a substantial dowry, however, to enter here as a choir nun."

Durant frowned. "I may find her reaction odd, but my curiosity about her past is unseemly. I do grieve that I so terrified her that she fainted."

"And she may well forget it soon enough. How do you feel now?"

"Exhausted." The wine merchant smiled to blunt the sharp honesty, but his gaze at the distance back to his bed suggested how much he dreaded the return. "Sit closer, if you will, so I do not have to strain to see your face."

Thomas edged nearer. "Sister Anne swears that her diet and properly planned exercise will bring you greater health."

"Yet my years on this earth will be limited." Durant caressed the tonsure on Thomas's head.

"As is true of us all. You cannot be certain of the exact number. We are rarely given knowledge of how long our time here will be."

"Sweetly said, but I am at peace with death as long as I

can see you daily for holy counsel and have you by my side when my soul goes to judgment."

Thomas felt his heart sink but felt hope when Durant looked up at the ceiling and set his jaw with determination.

"I must have goals for the regaining of my strength," the wine merchant said. "It is winter, so I must remain inside, but might I truly hope for a walk to the bee hives by summer?"

"That is quite possible," Thomas replied with a relieved smile. "Sister Anne would not have encouraged the hope if it were unrealistic."

"Then help me stand. I shall count my own shuffles back to bed and memorize the number to see how quickly I progress."

As Thomas raised Durant to his feet, the man leaned against him and held on with as much strength as he could.

"Hold me close for a moment, just a moment." Durant's voice was muffled against Thomas's shoulder. "I love you more than life and, I fear, even God. I beg you to teach me how to banish the latter, but please let me keep my love for you. You know I shall not trouble you otherwise, even if I once longed to sin, for I am doomed to abstinence."

As Thomas hugged him, he murmured something he hoped was a response in accordance with the terms of his penance. Durant might eschew all love making, but the monk knew that his own body would continue to torment him. Out of determination to fulfill the demands of his penance and give Durant the chance of Heaven, he would control his earthly longings and teach his beloved how to eventually face God. As he breathed in the comforting scent of the wine merchant, he could not keep back the surprising tears of joy as he held Durant closer. Even if they could not bond as one in bed, there was no question that he must have

Durant in his life no matter what the cost. They were one being in ways he could not explain and perhaps did not even want to do.

13

Sister Anne had just told her prioress that the cause of death was as simple as she had first observed. What roused her curiosity now were the possible circumstances surrounding the murder.

"From the way she fell, she must have seen her killer before the knife plunged into her heart. The attempt to keep the weapon from entering the body is a natural gesture, however useless it might be. Yet her hands were inexplicably free of cuts. Most would have screamed or cried out for help or held out a hand against the knife. If she did not, why?"

Eleanor felt as if her mind was ploughing through one of those deep snowdrifts that often buried priory land in winter. It was the common aftermath of her headaches. "No one from the priory has come to tell me of anything seen or heard. The chapel used by my cousin's wife is unavailable to the village and unknown to most lay visitors. It is used by us on rare occasion when a religious needs utter silence to communicate with God over some profound problem. My cousin knew of it only because I had given him permission to pray there when he needed the solitude. As for calling out, perhaps she did not have time. I agree that a passing religious could have heard a scream."

"Then Ralf need not question villagers?"

Eleanor was grateful that her headache was vanishing. Deep fatigue was approaching, but she willed herself to accomplish something before giving into sleep. "He may if he sees fit," she replied, "but I agree with you that there is little need. Of the few strangers here, I know of none likely to know the location of the place or have any reason to use it if they did. There are chapels enough for them in the public church."

"The maid and the priest?" Sister Anne tilted her head. "What of them?"

"Of course he will speak with them." Eleanor noted that her friend had not mentioned David. The omission curiously annoyed her. Was Sister Anne pretending that her cousin could not possibly be a suspect? Or was the sub-infirmarian afraid Eleanor could not face that he was? Both conclusions were insulting.

Perhaps it was her deepening weariness, but she was feeling unusually irritable. That David was possibly withholding the truth from her was so unnecessary. What could he possibly think was so important to hide that he was willing to let himself be the most obvious suspect for this murder? Her face grew numb with fear as she also forced herself to face the question of whether or not he was the killer.

"Now that I am through with the corpse, I will question the nuns and lay sisters if you wish."

"I would be grateful. At least I can depend on you to do so with efficiency and thoroughness."

Sister Anne nodded with pleasure at the compliment. "I

assume Prior Vincent will speak to the lay brothers and monks?"

"Prior Andrew would have asked Brother Beorn to help question the lay brothers, and I would have a report before the next Office." She struck the bed with her fist.

Sister Anne started at the unexpected violence of the gesture.

"May God forgive me for constantly being unfair to the man! He has his virtues, yet not the same ones I trusted Prior Andrew to perform. But that is another issue, and I simply need patience. Now! What more on this foul murder?"

"I admit that the chapel is not used much, the weather is chill, and mortals are less likely to pick that cold stone floor on which to kneel when warmer locations can be found for prayers. That the countess was seen is probably unlikely. But a scream? A cry for help? That could have been heard by anyone nearby but out of sight, or even by the lady's maid and priest. We can still hope for evidence of that."

"Might she have had her mouth bound or held shut?" Eleanor's eyes felt like boulders, and she was losing her fight against sleep. She knew the sub-infirmarian was aware of her headache and the phases as she recovered. Although Eleanor knew she was being unfair, she was growing impatient with Sister Anne for pursuing this discussion now. She knew all she had to do was tell her friend of the desperate need to sleep. As her eyes grew heavier, she had no energy left to ask and longed to have the nun realize her state without having to mention it.

"No evidence of bruising, scratches around the face, or a cloth burn. Nor did she seem to have scratched her killer. When that occurs, there is often flesh left under the victim's nails. The countess had longish ones, but I found no evidence of clawed skin or even a hint of blood. Nor were any nails broken, as there might be with a struggle. The latter therefore seems unlikely. As I noted, there was no bruising to suggest such either."

"It was almost as if she had wished for the death."

"It was not self-murder. The angle of the knife entry..."

"Yet she seemed to have allowed the blow as if she welcomed it. Or else she was too shocked by the attack to react as we might expect."

"Is it possible that she recognized the knife?" Sister Anne grew sad, and Eleanor grasped the true meaning of the question.

"I would not be offended if you asked whether my cousin might be the murderer," Eleanor replied curtly. "Of course he is a suspect. The knife is his. The relationship between him and his wife was a cool one, yet I know of no reason why he would have killed her. He was also with me for some time before word was sent of Eda's death." She saw her friend about to comment and held up her hand. "I am not saying he could not have had time to kill her before meeting me.The exact time of death cannot be determined. We have so many questions to answer. As for Eda being able to identify the knife, she would not have recognized the weapon if her first sight of it was while the hilt was hidden by a hand."

"And only a fool would use his own knife and leave it in the body."

Or else a clever man who knew others would dismiss his guilt because they knew he would not have been so stupid? Eleanor was not oblivious to the possible use of a fine trick. "He was very upset when he learned his knife had been stolen and used against his wife." She felt the jagged edge of anger as she fully realized where this discussion was leading. Of course she must be objective, but she also felt family loyalty.

Sister Anne smiled. "At least you will not be involved. Surely Ralf will be back from Norwich by tomorrow. He is rarely there for a long time, and he will take over the investigation since no one in the priory is suspect. I am sure he can clear your cousin of any involvement very quickly."

"The investigation remains my responsibility," Eleanor replied sharply. She did not even try to blunt her outrage. First, Sister Anne had insulted her by suggesting she either did not fully grasp her cousin's possible involvement or else that she was incapable of even imagining it. Now the nun was dismissing Eleanor's right to decide who had investigative responsibility!

The sub-infirmarian stiffened in surprise at her friend's tone and expression.

"The murder happened in this priory. Until I can prove that no one here was involved, Ralf has no authority to lead any investigation on God's land."

"He should at least question your cousin..."

"Nor will he be allowed to do so." Eleanor stood and hid her clenched hands in her sleeves. "I will be in complete charge until I deem it unnecessary."

Seeing the scowl on Prioress Eleanor's face as she rose, Sister Anne realized she had just been dismissed. Never had she been treated so coldly in the thirteen years of their friendship. She rose, understanding that any further discussion was over.

"Now I must attend to other tasks I have had to set aside due to this crime." Eleanor turned to the accounts rolled up on a nearby table. "I know I shall hear a report soon on your talks with the nuns and lay sisters here."

"Yes, my lady," Sister Anne said, then fled from the room.

Any tears due to the manner in which she had been treated would wait until she could escape to the nighttime privacy of her apothecary hut next to the hospital. But what troubled her especially was not knowing why this had even happened.

14

The morning light arrived dressed in gray. The sun never shone through. Instead, snow drifted down on all God's creation with a lethal cold.

The crowner rode through the gates of Tyndal Priory in a mood that matched the grim day. He had hoped to spend longer in bed with his wife after his return late last night from Norwich and was not well pleased to learn a slaying at the priory must drag him from her sweet warmth into this bitter chill. Looking around at the bone-white earth and the twisted black branches of trees, he saw no reason to think his spirits would lighten.

When he entered the quarters of Prioress Eleanor, he was given all due courtesy but none of the warm welcome he always received after an absence. Even Sister Anne failed to smile, keeping her head down and staying some distance from both him and the prioress. Odd as well was the absence of any attendant to bring food and drink. Eleanor herself poured a mazer of wine from a nearby ewer and put the cup down within reach of the crowner. He noticed that Sister Anne was not offered anything, nor did she hold a cup. He shivered, although the drink thawed him. The atmosphere, despite the crackling fire, was as hostile as the North Sea wind outside.

In all the years he had known Prioress Eleanor, he had seen her grow from a young woman of surprising talents and insights into a figure of whom myths are often made and even saints. Her manner was habitually quiet and thoughtful as befitted a religious, yet she also possessed an earthy laughter and wit. The worldly soon learned that she was no innocent who could be easily gulled and that she would quickly strip them of their gaudy pretensions. She was loyal to those she loved, forgave their many flaws, and was not prone to cruelty. Unlike some churchmen Ralf had met, his brother, the Abbot Odo, among them, she did not make God into a mirror image of human intolerance, wrath, and cruelty. Her God was a loving one.

Today, as she explained to him the known details of the murder committed in her priory chapel, he saw unexpected hints of a far different woman. The lines in her forehead were deeper than usual. Her gray eyes, which normally sparkled with merriment or darkened when faced with human cruelty, resembled the flat gaze of someone who was weary and had seen too much. She gestured little and stood stiffly. Never once did she turn to her friend Sister Anne to provide detail as she was wont to do. The absence of Brother Thomas was also unusual. Even the cat was missing.

Prioress Eleanor now ended her recitation of the facts and fell silent. Her eyes focused on him with an intensity that might have drilled a hole through him had her gaze been a carpenter's auger.

"Thank you, my lady," he said, his speech more formal than usual to match the unusual tension in the room. "I am grateful for the information you have gained. It will save me much time in the investigation." He looked at Sister Anne.

She had yet to lift her head.

"Our sub-infirmarian will take you to view the body," Eleanor said. Her tone was abrupt and dismissive.

"It is most unfortunate that this crime occurred here and troubled you and your flock, especially so soon before the Christmas season." He bowed. "I will work with you so anything I or my men must do here in this investigation will cause the least amount of disruption. From what you have said, however, this murder falls into the realm of the king's jurisdiction. No one at the priory has been involved."

"I must disagree," she said, her voice dropping in pitch to one that closely resembled a growl. "This murder occurred on God's land. Until I have established that no one under His law has any part in the crime, the process and responsibility of this investigation remain mine."

Although Ralf had always respected her decisions on jurisdiction and eagerly welcomed her help in cases under the king's law, he was surprised at this unbending tone. After all, there was one very obviously troubling aspect of this case, and he was shocked that she either did not see the problem or had uncharacteristically chosen to ignore it. Her cousin.

"As you will, my lady," he said, trying to banish from his speech any traces that betrayed the depth of his dismay. "But your cousin, although surely as innocent as you or I, is a suspect. That investigation must be done by me. As you know...you...well, I mean..." He stopped before he embarrassed himself even further with his inability to say what he meant. Diplomacy had never been one of his strengths.

"You accuse me of lack of objectivity?"

In the past, she would have said that with an amused tone. Ralf felt only chill. He simply nodded.

"You are, of course, free to think what you will. But my decision to remain in charge of this investigation is unchanged. That includes the choice of who will interview whom and how any suspect is handled. I am not saying that you and your men cannot contribute to the hunt for the killer. There were many strangers here at the time. As always, I welcome your thoughts, and I expect to be promptly and fully informed of any discoveries made by you. But I shall direct what you and your men do on priory land."

Although a tiny woman, Ralf thought, her steely determination gave her a presence that overpowered everyone in the room. "As you wish," he said, "but your cousin..."

As if fighting back fierce anger, she hissed, "My cousin is the Earl of Ness."

Had Ralf had not lost his breath from the shock of hearing her use her cousin's rank as an excuse to give him leniency, he would have gasped. Instead, his own temper sparked, and his face felt hot. Had Prioress Eleanor been an ordinary mortal, he would have roared oaths that were sharper than any whip.

"Sister Anne?"

The nun looked up for the first time. "Yes, my lady?"

"Take our crowner to view the body. I shall summon you both at a later time when I am ready to hear any thoughts you might have." With that, Prioress Eleanor spun on her heel and marched into her private chambers, slamming the door behind her.

Ralf looked at Sister Anne and opened his mouth.

"Later, Ralf," she murmured. "The corpse takes precedence. Then we can speak."

The two left the chambers. As they did, Arthur marched past them without a glance.

Ralf stopped to watch him and noted that the door to the private chamber was opening ever so slightly. The admission of the cat to the private quarters gave him some comfort after this strange meeting. At least something remained familiar on this very unnatural day.

15

—————

Brother Thomas had not slept well the previous night. He had expected bad dreams because of his profound doubt about his ability to help Durant gain his desired purity. What he had not expected was that he would be sent back to that time when he was raped in prison. Each remembered detail slowed down so he not only suffered them again but with greater agony. Those he had gratefully been able to banish were recalled with vivid brutality.

At the time, he had struggled and screamed when his jailers held him down. In his dream, however, he was paralyzed and his voice silenced. The only sound he heard was the mocking laughter of those watching while the chief jailer rutted and grunted. When Thomas finally woke, sweating in the icy air, he wept from the pain his body had never forgotten. The nightmares had been so vivid he was shocked he wasn't lying in his own blood again.

He then forced himself to rise, wash, and will himself to go back to Durant with renewed determination, but the night would not release him that easily. He stopped on the path and pressed his hand to his pounding heart. Was this

God's way of telling him that the penance ordered by Brother John was beyond his ability to achieve, that he must go to the hermit and beg another way to cleanse his soul? Or was it Satan, reminding him yet again of the mockery he was as both man and monk? And how many more times must he be given a foretaste of Hell?

"Are you ill, Brother?" The voice was unfamiliar but soft and concerned.

A strong odor overwhelmed Thomas even before his eyes focused on Father Fithian, the dead countess's priest, standing in front of him. The reek emanating from the priest was a mix of accumulated sweat, stale urine, and fresh feces. Thomas lowered his head as his stomach began to churn.

"A momentary pain, now vanished," he replied, determined to change the subject. "I regret that your arrival here was greeted with such violence, Father. You must be grieving over the death of the countess." He looked up and concentrated on the priest's eyes. "Had you served long as her spiritual advisor?"

"Many years. I returned with her brother when he came back from the Crusades." Father Fithian spoke as if the memory were a mix of bitter and sweet.

"You spent time in the Holy Land?"

"The knight in whose household I served had gone there, and I followed. He died there. When he did, I realized I missed Scotland and longed to return home. When the countess's brother offered me passage with him, I accepted."

Thomas felt oddly drawn to this man. There was a quietness about him that he envied. Yet he was also attracted to his gentle and seemingly caring manner. His awareness of the reek slowly faded as he began to study the priest in more detail.

Fithian's voice was higher in pitch than most men's but

pleasant to the ear. His lips, Thomas noted, were fuller than men commonly owned, but his face was square and lean. Although Father Fithian did not bathe, his face was remarkably close-shaven, his brown hair clean, and his tonsure neatly trimmed. He sensed the priest had suffered something deeply wounding in his past. If true, he had survived it with kindness instead of hate, as too many did. Thomas wondered if Father Fithian might teach him wisdom from any trials he had endured, something he could pass on to others—or even a way to deal with his own agonies.

Suddenly, Thomas realized he had been staring and tried to blink as if something had flown into his eye. "How came you to serve his sister instead?"

Father Fithian tilted his head as if amused by Thomas's obvious attempt to hide his thoughts, but his smile conveyed understanding.

"Forgive me. My curiosity is unseemly," Thomas said as an apology.

"I do not think it is, Brother. Of course you would ask questions. Your reputation as a hunter of murderers is well-known."

The remark was intended to sound like a compliment, but Thomas felt a bite in it. Annoyance? Had the priest been insulted? Or had he felt threatened? Suddenly, Thomas realized that the tone was most akin to the weariness of someone all too accustomed to being questioned. "I did not intend to interrogate you," he quickly replied, but his curiosity was now set fully ablaze.

"Ask what you will, Brother. If I can provide any information that helps bring the murderer to earthly justice, I long to do so, even though I fear I have nothing to offer."

Thomas grinned like a boy caught too many times stealing a treat from the kitchen but who still hoped to escape punishment. "You are kind, and I confess that I am

86

curious. Since you have known the countess for so long, might there have been a particular enemy who wanted to kill her? No matter how good a person may be, there is usually someone who is less than charmed."

"That is a question I cannot answer with certitude, and I would be ill-advised to offer conjectures. I have no wish to cast an unfair shadow on any innocent. The fewer of us who do that, the better. I am sure the local crowner is a busy man and does not wish to be distracted by unsound imaginings."

"I understand, Father, but your words suggest you might have suspicions. Please speak freely. I will treat your thoughts with caution and respect."

With a somber gaze, Father Fithian looked around at the priory buildings. "The crime may have been committed here, but surely there is no reason to think the killer is one of your monastics?" He sighed. "I am sure Prioress Eleanor will surrender her authority to the king's law, and I only pray that our party of weary travelers may leave for Scotland soon."

What an odd reply, Thomas thought. Was he hinting that he had some knowledge, or was he simply hoping to deflect queries directed solely to the traveling party of the Earl of Ness? "You are wise not to chatter about what might or might not have happened, Father. As for the authority to investigate, I do not know if it has been decided. Crowner Ralf has arrived and will confer with Prioress Eleanor."

"Then I must continue on my way to pray. I believe the bell rang for the Office."

Thomas nodded. He longed to continue his conversation with the priest but dared not keep him from prayer.

The priest bowed his head with courtesy and left.

Watching him, Thomas sensed that the man had suddenly felt a need to flee, although he had seemed in control for most of their talk. As Father Fithian vanished,

Thomas became aware again of his stench and that it was dissipating. His head hurt from the reek.

Hardworking men smelled of sweat, but it was from the day's labor and often washed off with a swim on hot days, he thought. The old might wet themselves, and the sick lose control of their bowels. In the priory hospital, both were cleansed at Sister Anne's orders. Only those cursed with twisted wits or those who rejected any form of bathing as an evil luxury let their bodies get this encrusted with filth. Thankfully, the latter were usually hermits who fled any human contact.

But Father Fithian was not a desert father, nor was he sick, elderly, or bereft of sense. Indeed, from the neck up, he was clean and neat, almost to the point of vanity. The reason probably had nothing to do with murder, but Thomas's curious mind liked satisfying even when a crime was not an issue. There was so much about the man that piqued Thomas's interest.

Yet murder was an issue. Might Father Fithian be less concerned about the lethal potential of idle gossip and more about hiding guilt for himself or another? Had he hated the woman for whom he was the spiritual advisor? Why did he draw away from any detailed answers about his past, no matter how innocuous the question? He might be a man who preferred not to talk about himself, a humility certainly proper to his calling, but it was an equally logical conclusion that he was hiding something of importance.

Priests were not immune to worldly temptations or earthly faults. High-ranking churchmen often lived in opulent manors, making a mockery out of the simple life of the founder of the faith. Priests and bishops openly lived with women and did not deny that the resultant progeny were theirs. But murder? There were tales enough about such things committed among men in high position, but would a simple priest kill the person to whom he had been giving spiritual direction for years?

The answer, he knew full well, was that almost anything was possible. One of the first murders he and his prioress solved together involved a religious who had committed a brutal murder. Yet Father Fithian did not seem like an evil man or one who had worldly ambitions. In fact, he appeared to be retiring and quiet, a man who wished most to pray and keep the world at arm's length. If the latter, why had he not become a monk? That was a thought he set aside for deliberation were it to become relevant as opposed to mere trifling curiosity.

"So is Father Fithian a killer, or is it only his stench that might be lethal?" He tried to chuckle at his weak attempt at humor but failed. The man appealed to him for reasons he could not quite define, a feeling he must set aside if he was obliged to include him in any investigation of the crime.

But he suspected it was most likely that the murder would belong to the crowner despite occurring on priory ground. Even though Ralf would work closely with Prioress Eleanor until it was decided that the perpetrator was a secular person and not one vowed to the Church, Thomas believed he would have little part in investigating.

Yet he still wondered why the crime had taken place here and why it had happened in that little chapel.

16

―――――

"Why?" the crowner roared as he slammed his fist down on a nearby railing. He had successfully managed to remain silent until he and Sister Anne arrived at the hospital chapel and she had finished explaining what had happened between her and the prioress.

"Hush, Ralf." The sub-infirmarian glanced around, but no one seemed to be within hearing except for the Countess of Ness. Her corpse, now lying close to the cross, had clearly lost all interest in petty human concerns.

Glancing heavenward, as if apologizing to God for breaking a holy silence, he lowered his voice to a rough hiss. "You have been her confidant from the beginning, loved as much as any sister who shared the same mother's womb, and respected for your apothecary skills, which have helped her solve crimes."

"And she snapped at you like many of rank do men of little worth. I heard her tone and saw her face."

Ralf shook his head like a dog with a flea in the ear, then looked as if he were ready to start on a lengthy rant.

Sister Anne raised a finger. "Yet..."

Not only did Ralf stop in mid-word, he shoved his jaw up with his hand to force his mouth shut.

"...we must forgive her."

"I concede that you might, Annie. You have the makings of sainthood within you, but I am a rude man of secular habits and less inclined to kindness or turning my bristled cheek. And do not argue! You have known me since we were both children and are well acquainted with my failings." He turned away so she would not see him blush. Included in those frailties were the many years he had hopelessly loved her despite her marriage to another and entry to Tyndal Priory.

"I need say nothing," Sister Anne said with a gentle tone. "Your wife and children can testify to your secret kindness and loving nature." Then she laughed. "As for sainthood, I know you have no inclination there. Gytha has told me enough to make me quite aware of your mutual joy when you return home after even a short absence."

This time, Ralf could do nothing to hide his red face. He might have glowed in the dark with embarrassment.

"But you do not know all our prioress has been dealing with since her return last year after our escape from Wales and the murders in that border town."

He shrugged, but his expression relayed his willingness to listen despite the dismissive gesture.

"You are aware that this killing is the second murder she has had to face since then. Prior Andrew has died. Prior Vincent was elected by the monks but does not have the talents or good nature of Prior Andrew. Much of the work done by our beloved former prior has now fallen on her until the new prior gains expertise, if he indeed ever does. Sister Ruth has suffered apoplexy..."

"I see, but..."

"Sister Gracia has joined the choir nuns and is learning

91

how to do several tasks that will allow her to take on greater responsibility as her skills demand."

He tried to wave that problem aside. "She could have remained in service to Prioress Eleanor."

"As she wanted, but our prioress said she had too many abilities to do so. The priory needs must come first, so she insisted Sister Gracia take other work. That meant someone else had to take the young woman's place. That was Sister Serena, a young nun who has proven herself to be anything but serene. You noticed that our prioress herself served us?"

"If you can call it that. No food. A little liquid to..."

"Your stomach may be what keeps you out of Heaven, Ralf. Sister Serena had begged time for prayer in the chapel in penance for spilling a goblet of wine in the rushes. Her request was probably granted as much to give our prioress some peace as it was to soothe the young woman's soul."

Ralf could not resist a grin. "That bad, is she?"

"But I am not finished with the list of trials our prioress endures. You cannot dismiss what it means that Sister Ruth is coming to the end of her earthly days after her recent attack of apoplexy. How quickly may remain in question, but her health declines steadily. She may have been the cause of much anxiety in the past, but Prioress Eleanor respected her talents and grieves already for her loss. There is much the two women need to settle between them quickly. How to do so remains the responsibility of Prioress Eleanor."

The sub-infirmarian sighed. "To be brief, Ralf, our prioress needs a sub-prioress to help her with all the work she now must do herself as well as a prior who quickly learns his duties so she doesn't have to do his work as well. The former may be found. The latter may never happen. She is exhausted and now must contend with a murder in which her beloved cousin is a prime suspect."

"And that is the problem, Annie. She wants to take on the investigation but should not do so. How can she not be prejudiced in her cousin's favor? Earl of Ness? Fa! When a crime has been committed, all I know is that an earl pisses against walls like any other man. I have seen my elder brother of good rank do the same and my abhorred second brother, a fine abbot, squat behind a bush too small to hide his ample buttocks."

Sister Anne folded her arms. "I am relieved to hear this speech! That is the Ralf I know. Since you have finally recovered from the failure of anyone to offer you a round of local cheese and a loaf of Sister Matilda's fresh bread, maybe you can also set aside the snappishness of an exhausted prioress and concentrate on the details of murder."

He looked as if he were ready to argue, then nodded solemnly. "Very well, Annie. If you can forgive the insults, then I can do the same for far lesser cause. Now tell me more about the corpse."

It did not take long.

"The weapon belongs to the Earl of Ness?" Ralf scowled.

"Which he freely admits. Brother Thomas went with the earl to search the man's quarters. As expected, the knife was missing."

"The earl does not know who might have taken it or when?"

"Questions you had best ask yourself. I was not told."

"Did he recognize the jeweled crucifix?"

"Our prioress did not say before our quarrel. Perhaps she hasn't asked him, or she might have decided to hide his answer. I am not ignoring the likelihood she wants to protect him out of familial love, Ralf. I am only counseling tact with her and that we listen to her reasons. She has proven herself to be both wise and just over many years, has she not?"

He frowned. "You say the countess fell as if facing her killer, so she must have recognized him. You also wonder, as do I, why she did not cry out, even if no one else was in the chapel at the same time. It would be natural for a victim to do that as well as try to keep the knife from entering the chest."

"No defensive wounds. No one has come forth to tell of hearing a scream. Prior Vincent found the body, sent word to our prioress and to me, and then kept the curious away. He will question the monks and lay brothers."

Ralf snorted. "That might take months. If Signy would agree, I'd set Nute to the task. He'd be done in a day, and Brother Beorn would help with the lay brothers. Secular lad though he is, he is observant and well liked in the priory." He looked sad. "But I cannot give orders to a prior, and, no matter what, Prioress Eleanor is unlikely to give me much latitude."

"I have taken responsibility for questioning the nuns and lay sisters and have already sent word to Sister Gracia to query the nuns. As soon as I can return to the hospital, I will arrange for Sister Oliva to do as much as she can at the apothecary so I can speak with the lay sisters."

"At least that will all be done efficiently and thoroughly."

"Prior Vincent may surprise us both, Ralf. He has been in the priory for many years. He was here when I arrived. The men did respect him enough to elect him their prior. Surely that proves he has ability and personal merit."

He did not retort that he thought she was being too kind again. Instead, he asked, "What other monk was considered?"

"I do not know, nor would I. I can only treat the monks at a distance under the rules of our vows and must leave their direct care to our talented medical lay brothers. That situation does not allow me to learn much about the organizational qualifications of our brothers on the other side of the priory."

He hesitated. "Did Brother Thomas vote for him?"

"I would never ask."

"Very well, Annie." Ralf laughed. "I will cease my prying of you. But now we must find a way to work around our exhausted but stubborn prioress in this matter of her cousin." His countenance soured again.

"I suspect that she will call for us both quite soon and apologize. After all, you noted that Arthur was allowed into her private rooms. By now, she will have talked to him, and he always gives her good counsel." She chuckled. "Fortunately, I believe you are in favor with the cat, so he might speak well on your behalf."

Ralf bit his tongue before he uttered something scornful in response and continued to remain silent as he followed the sub-infirmarian out of the hospital chapel.

17

Eleanor was no longer talking to her cat. Instead, she was kneeling in front of the altar at the priory church where Prior Andrew had been buried in a place of honor.

"I miss you," she said, sitting back on her heels. "But you had suffered far too long with that old wound. It is selfish of me to wish you were still on earth, but my better nature is grateful you are no longer in pain. You were a good man, and God has surely rewarded you with a place by His side."

She fell silent, not because she believed Prior Andrew's spirit would respond, but rather to honor the position she was convinced he must now hold in the afterlife.

Tears stung her eyes. Many of these were born of grief from the death of her beloved prior. Occasionally, she asked God if it was wicked to weep when a person died, even though they were now in Heaven. Yet she knew it was the nature of mortals to do so and suspected God understood pain over losing someone who had brought comfort in a wicked world. "Sorrow over the loss of a loved one does not preclude rejoicing because they now stand with God." Her words were not meant to persuade Him that she owned a strong faith. They were her way of assuring herself that one could hold two conflicting emotions in the heart.

The tears over Prior Andrew would surely last a lifetime, but the ones she now began to shed had a different cause.

"I have been cruel to those I love," she whispered in confession. "Neither Ralf nor Anne deserved my wicked arrogance. Yes, I am weary with the trials of a maid who is not like my beloved Gytha or Gracia. Prior Vincent dislikes me as much as I do him. He does not match Prior Andrew in skill, so I must hover over his work like a hawk. He resents my interference yet never sees the many errors he makes."

She stopped, knowing she was just repeating a litany of complaints for which time and cool reason must be found in order to resolve. Her teeth were clenched, and she slowly forced herself to relax. "I have been most fortunate in my time leading this priory to enjoy the competence of godly men and women," she said as she struggled to claw her way to greater objectivity. "Have You decided it was time I learned patience? Or humility? Or kindness under duress? . Most likely, all three?" She smiled, knowing that Prior Andrew would have too if he were still on earth.

Moving back to the kneeling position, Eleanor folded her hands and again fell into silent prayer. She cast set phrases aside, having already uttered all those demanded of the pious, and tried to open her soul to the answers she longed for.

She had always been drawn to the story of Moses and the burning bush in the desert. Before God had spoken, there was silence. In that, she often thought, lay the crux of the wisdom sought. She must leave it to priests to find the words to explain what that silence meant. As a woman, she could only hope that, surrounded by profound stillness, God would fill her with that peace that also passeth all understanding.

97

High in the roof of the chapel, a wintering bird chirped and was answered by one of his fellows some distance away. The chill wind outside may have lessened in force, but the air inside the chapel had not warmed. With more than a hint of deadly intent, the sharp cold circled her bare hands and tried to slip into the space between the woolen cloth of her sleeves and her arms.

For a very long time, Eleanor remained oblivious to any such earthly distraction.

At last, she opened her eyes and stood. "Thank you," she said with a bow to the altar and reluctantly turned to leave.

"Patience it is, then," she whispered to herself. "Prior Vincent has been with the Order for years. He was duly elected prior by his fellow monks. There is a reason. I must simply find it and grow accustomed to how he works." She looked back over her shoulder. "I shall continue to miss you, Prior Andrew, but I will learn to banish my selfish impatience with your successor."

As she stepped outside, she also swore aloud to be kinder to Sister Serena. "The nun is not lazy or wicked. She wants to serve. I cannot keep comparing her to Gytha and Gracia, both of whom own my heart. I could have kept Gracia at my side, but she is clever and capable. Not to offer her skills to the running of Tyndal would have been sinful."

With no warning, Eleanor slipped and almost fell on the snowy path. As she righted herself, she remembered one more thing she had failed to do. "I must visit Sister Ruth without further delay," she said and vowed not to set this task aside much longer. No matter what trials each had caused the other, the women had learned wary but dutiful and mutual respect. There had never been love or even a vague fondness between them, but Eleanor could not let the nun go to God without letting her know how much she had appreciated her talents and holy service. It would be a grave sin to fail to confess her honest gratitude.

Walking head down to avoid another fall and deep in thought, she did not at first see the two men in conversation nearby. When she became aware, she paused. She doubted either could see her behind the clump of winter-blasted shrubbery along the path so she chose to watch for a moment.

Brother Thomas was talking with Father Fithian.

The good monk always knew what she needed before she asked, she thought, and was likely seeking information from the man.

Pressing her hand to her heart, she whispered to God that she was grateful she still had him at her side. All of the reasons Brother John had decided her monk must care for the wine merchant were still unknown, but the hermit had said that lessons in selfless love were the greatest weapons against human evil. That message applied to her as well as her monk, and she decided it was well to remind herself of it when she was falling short herself. Of late, she had certainly failed far more than usual.

Knowing that Brother Thomas would report what he had learned from this conversation with Father Fithian, she walked briskly away to her chambers.

Then she stopped and looked back. Hadn't she ordered Father Fithian to remain in his room until she called for him? She had not sent Sister Serena. Maybe Brother Thomas had released him for a walk so he could question the man? Yet she had not sent the monk, and it was unlikely he would have gone to interrogate the priest without talking to her first. This meeting must have been accidental. Worried, she took a couple of steps toward the men, then changed her mind.

"Brother Thomas will explain all to me soon," she

murmured. She had always trusted him to do the right things. As for Father Fithian's disobedience, this might not be a willful disregard of her command. He might have had cause. Indeed, she knew of no reason to think all was not well now.

With that thought, she journeyed back to her quarters. She had much to do, beginning with apologies to both Sister Anne and Crowner Ralf.

Some might claim that as the head of Tyndal, respected by many including Queen Eleanor, she had no need to do this, but Eleanor disagreed. Pride was certainly one of her many failings, but she knew humility was demanded by her vocation. When all of us face God, she thought, there will be no distinctions in rank or gender, only whether each of us has honored the Ten Commandments as well as the eleventh—that we must love our neighbors as ourselves.

Meanwhile, she had a worldly problem to solve as well as her spiritual ones.

She must find a way to convince Ralf that she had to control this investigation. Of course she was prejudiced in favor of her cousin, but she knew that. If David was guilty, however, she wanted to be the one to lead him to justice and remain by his side for any punishment. He was her family. More than that, he was so much like his mother, who had raised her. She owed it to Sister Beatrice's soul to guarantee that David's innocence or guilt be determined fairly and with love.

She had snapped at Ralf that her cousin was the Earl of Ness. She had not meant that his rank protected him from any consequences of guilt. It was intended to explain that David was unaccustomed to being questioned by most men, but as his cousin, she could do what others could not. If he was hiding something, either his own involvement or out of a wish to protect others, she would be in the best position to drag out the truth. David would resist Ralf to the death, even if that death were unwarranted. He would try to resist her too, but she had learned to read his soul's secrets many years ago. He could never hold out against her for long.

With a greater feeling of confidence about the route she must take despite the normally valid argument against it that Ralf would make, she knew she would find a way to force her cousin to confide in her. She was probably more aware than anyone, except Brother Thomas, that her cousin was not telling the whole truth. "Actually," she said in a low voice, "David is not just avoiding details, I know he is lying."

Close behind her, Eleanor heard the loud crunching sound of someone running toward her in the frozen snow. She looked behind her and winced despite her fine resolve mere moments ago.

Prior Vincent approached, his expression sour and his arm stretched high as he waved a parchment roll in his hand.

"Charity," she groaned to the heavens, then forced her expression into one she prayed would be an adequate portrayal of welcome or at least of calm.

Snowflakes, delicate and fresh, began to fall again on all creatures that inhabited the shivering earth. Whatever else evil might concoct, even the weather seemed eager to add yet more misery to the unfolding events.

18

Having resolved her prior's latest quandary and now gratefully back in her warm chambers, Eleanor watched from her window as the snow fell with solemn determination and deadly charm.

Her mood darkened.

How many mortals had grown sleepy in the cold, curled up in a solitary spot, and died in the bewitching embrace of such perfect beauty?

She closed the shutters and rested her hand for a long time on the rough wood of the slats. How many of these acts were intentional self-murder, a grave transgression sometimes known only to God?

The peace from her recent prayers was fading, but she was well aware that giving in to despair was unacceptable. Although she had never wished to commit self-murder, she understood the dark grief of the hopeless. Since Prior Andrew's death, she had been unable to shake off the pressures of her problems. It had been far easier when she was younger. Now she was more prone to bursts of anger and impatience. Or was it mostly the loss of his support and friendship? She knew she had depended on him, but perhaps she had never realized quite how much.

She shook her head. Of course she had been a green child when she took over Tyndal, but she had been trained by her aunt on how to read mortal souls and take on responsibility. These were lessons she relished. No, the problem lay in the number of unwelcome changes and problems that had occurred in the short time between their unfortunate journey to Wales and the return here.

She still wondered why so much had happened. Had she committed sins of which even she was unaware and for which she must be very severely punished? A priest could reveal those errors as she confessed, and she would willingly serve penance. However, the worst sins of all, as far as she was concerned, were the wounds she had inflicted on two of her dearest friends. She had treated them with a caustic arrogance so ugly she did not even recognize herself as the one who had been that cruel. She wanted to cry but knew that was self-indulgent. Blaming Satan suggested she owned less responsibility than she did.

Ralf and Sister Anne now waited in her audience chamber. She could hear their voices. It was time to bend her stiff neck and humble herself as she ought.

Turning to open the door, she swooped up her sleeping cat with her other hand and held him near to give her courage. She was ready to greet Sister Anne and Crowner Ralf with remorse and shame and to beg forgiveness, but had her cruelty left permanent scars on these two people who did not deserve them?

Sister Anne laughed when she saw her prioress carrying the huge tabby. Even Ralf grinned.

"My beloved friends! I brought Arthur here to help prove how deeply troubled I am with the weight of my sins against you. Were he to speak, he would be eloquent on my behalf in begging forgiveness for the way I have treated you both. He has heard me say at my prie-dieu how profoundly I grieve over my words earlier."

She put the cat down on the floor, where he remained seated and gazed up at her with a perplexed expression.

"Well, I had hoped he might speak on my behalf," Eleanor said with a hand on her hip. "Instead, his silence confirms how unforgivably wicked I have been. So I can only point to my heart and swear that it was absent when I spoke as I did. The love I hold there for you two would never have allowed such vile and unwarranted speech."

Sister Anne walked to Eleanor, took her hands, and grasped them with affection. "How long have I known you?"

Eleanor bowed her head as she squeezed back. "Since my arrival in this priory. You have been my support in all matters and have given me strength."

"And I met you only a few days after when you were forced to deal with a foul murder." Ralf's face reddened. "I was a rude man with little interest in courtesy, assumed you were a witless child, and treated you with disrespect. From that day on, you have ignored my faults and showed me kindness."

Sister Anne looked over her shoulder. "You are still a rude man, Ralf, but since your wife, whom we all adore, finds merit in you, we must as well."

The crowner grunted, but it was clear that he knew the sub-infirmarian was teasing—mostly.

"Please sit, my friends, and let me serve you refreshment." Eleanor gestured to the bench near the table, picked up a ewer of wine, and then gave mazers of the vintage to each.

Sister Anne put down her cup and went to cut thick slices of Sister Matilda's bread. It was so fresh the odor still wafted through the room. "Where is Sister Serena?"

Ralf immediately brightened as the sub-infirmarian handed him an especially thick piece.

She winked at her old friend.

"She begged leave to pray in the chapel today," Eleanor said. "She is grieving over spilling that wine and wanted to serve penance. The accident was such a small thing, but I did not argue. It is easily forgotten by me, but she needed the comfort of prayer."

"And thus Ralf and I will also forget our last meeting here." Sister Anne glanced at the crowner and smiled, satisfied that he agreed. "We know how much you have been burdened since the return from Wales. Words spoken out of profound weariness have been swept like dust from our memories."

Ralf concurred.

The Prioress of Tyndal knelt in gratitude.

Sister Anne gasped and pulled her friend to her feet. "Let us return to what we must discuss!"

"Then I may say now what I meant before I snapped like a rabid dog?"

"Aye," they replied in unison.

"Ralf, I did not insist on leading this investigation because I wished to protect my cousin. Yes, he does hold a place in my heart, much like that of a brother. He reminds me a great deal of his mother, Sister Beatrice, who raised me at Amesbury with tenderness and wisdom, as you both know."

They murmured understanding.

"You fear that I have no objectivity with him and his possible involvement in murder. That is justified." Eleanor hesitated. "That acknowledged, I still feel I should be the one to lead the effort to find the killer of his wife." She looked at each of them, waiting for a response. When none came, she continued. "My cousin is unaccustomed to bowing to any man except the king of our country and that of Scotland. If questioned in this crime, he will resist out of habit and pride. Yet I hold a special place with him. If anyone can pry out the truth of what he knows, or even what he does not realize he knows, it is I." She hesitated. "One more detail in support of my belief that he will tell me the truth. He is the adoring son of the woman who raised me. Why would he kill his wife in a priory of which I am the head? If he wanted to murder her, he would have done so someplace else."

"Your points are well taken," Ralf said. "Yet we both know that this crime belongs to the king's justice. The murder victim was not a religious, nor is there any reason to suspect that one of your flock committed it. Perhaps you might question your cousin as you wish, but..."

"Have you found evidence that explains why this crime was committed here, Ralf, and not on the journey to the priory, for instance?"

"No, although you must concede that the location was probably convenient rather than any indication of guilt by a religious."

"I am not pointing a finger at anyone," Eleanor replied. "All I beg is that I be allowed to lead the inquiries for a brief time until I am satisfied that my priory owns no part in the murder other than, as you reasonably suggested, convenience."

Ralf did not say what he was thinking. To him, the likelihood of the killer being a monastic was ridiculous. And she might be more objective than most when a family member was a suspect in a killing, but he was not convinced that even she could be sufficiently lacking in blindness about the Earl of Ness.

Eleanor smiled. "I give you my word, Ralf, that I shall personally bring my cousin to you for chains if I discover he murdered his wife. And should I weaken in my resolve to probe his involvement with sharp persistence, I will surrender my authority to you immediately." She gestured at Sister Anne. "She will be honest enough to tell me, and I give you both my oath that I shall listen. Does that satisfy you, Ralf?"

He started. Was he that transparent in his thinking or did this woman simply know him all too well? He cleared his throat and replied, "I do fear that our king may find reason to quarrel with you and the Church if he discovers that one of his liegemen has been a suspect but not questioned by either crowner or sheriff."

"Nor will I allow you or your family to suffer any injury because I begged your kind indulgence in this matter," she said. "The time needed to accomplish my purpose will be very brief."

Ralf chose not to argue further. Had this been anyone other than Prioress Eleanor, he would have ordered her to step back and allow him take over what was clearly an investigation under the king's law. But his respect for her eclipsed all reasonable and conventional wisdom. She had sworn she would not take long, and although the reason she gave for taking any control might be questionable, he had enough years of experience with her to chance the latitude just given.

"Now," Eleanor said, finally pouring herself a little wine, "tell me your conclusions and ideas after viewing the corpse."

19

The snow ceased to fall, but night darkness brought clouds to obscure the sight of angels in the sky carrying those flickering torches to remind mortals of His love. Yet for many religious who had escaped to bone-warming fires and now held cups of mulled wine, the mounds of unblemished whiteness pleased the eye and even reminded some of the purity of chaste living.

Father Fithian saw none of the beauty as he hurried to his destination. To him, it was Satan's hour, a time of death. His only consolation—and his lips curled in brittle mirth at the thought—was that worms would be too frozen to eat his body until spring if he died now.

Despite his unease, he reminded himself that he had always been possessed by ardent faith. Had he not been, he would not be in this situation. He was trembling so much he could barely steady himself on the path. Yet it was not the icy air that caused his body to shake.

His small torch wavered and spat in the dampness, but he finally saw the stone building with the chapel he sought. Prioress Eleanor had forbidden him to leave his quarters, but she was wrong to do so. He had chosen this place deliberately for his prayers tonight. This chapel was where the countess had died. If her soul still hovered, he hoped God might allow her to reassure him—or at least clarify—how much danger he was in.

When he entered the room reserved for prayer, the silence closed in on him. It did not comfort. It felt like a noxious embrace. Yet someone had lit a few small cresset lamps. Was this because a murder had been committed here, or was the lighting a usual practice? He hoped that any demons would be kept far away by the sight of the holy altar. Satan's minions rarely hovered near crosses, but Fithian had reason to suspect that a few might still linger if their master demanded it.

He tried but could not quite vanquish his fear. Fithian decided he must take comfort in believing that he had the chapel to himself. No one was visible. Surely that meant no imps circled either.

With reverence, he approached the altar and knelt.

After reciting the set prayers for the hour, he began to implore God to be merciful to the countess's soul. This was difficult for him, but he knew God would credit his effort if not his complete commitment.

The Countess of Ness had been a hard woman for all her proclaimed piety. Some even whispered that her claimed reverence was a mockery because she was cruel and selfish. Fithian often clenched his jaw over her demands, but he concluded that God must have chosen such an arduous service as his penance for his uniquely egregious sins or else a great blessing. Others like him were not so fortunate, and he knew it. He had cause to be deeply grateful that God had shown kindness by allowing him to continue in His service as a priest despite what Fithian was and had done.

Again, the trembling struck him like an ague. But had

God finally decided to withdraw His protection? Had the countess revealed his terrible secrets, as she so often did, and was he doomed like other sinners to the pain of earthly punishment?

If only his loved benefactor had lived! The man had discovered his secret one unfortunate night and retreated in horror. Then Fithian had saved his life in the Holy Land with prayers and a strange poultice learned from an old Muslim physician. Out of gratitude, the crusader had swore never to reveal Fithian's secret. Indeed, he believed it was then that they came to love one another in spite of everything and coupled as a man and a woman despite being sworn to chastity and, in Fithian's case, his own unique vow. But he could not stop that fatal fever that had taken the man's soul to God, and he had no further wish to remain where memory of his loss was too cruel. The countess's brother had taken him back to Scotland and a brief period of service before that former crusader had died of a knife blow. But he had been especially kind, and before his death he had begged his sister to take Fithian on as her priest should he die, swearing he was a holy man and would guide her to Heaven. For many years, she had believed this and kept him in her service.

Then she had discovered his secret. Just recently, she called him to a private audience and told him what she had learned. The glee with which she announced the news made her otherwise plain face actually glow with a satanic beauty. But, as Fithian reminded himself, Satan had been one of God's most beautiful angels before he was cast into Hell.

With much pleasure, she told him that she would reveal his secret to the Church and he would be expelled. He had fallen to his knees, wept, and begged her not to do so out of mercy and the memory of her crusader brother. She laughed and claimed it was her sacred duty to do as she had said. Because of her piety, God had ordered her to reveal the wickedness of as many as possible so they might suffer the judgment of other men as a foretaste of eternal damnation.

He could no longer be a priest, a vocation he deeply longed to follow, nor would he even be allowed to retreat to a priory. He would be forced to beg alms where no one had ever heard of him. He would die of cold and starvation on some Scottish heath. He could not escape to the Continent either, for his sin was so terrible that all monasteries and churches would know of his crimes.

Now he looked up, over the figure on the cross that stretched above the altar, and into the impenetrable gloom that lay beyond the circle of the dark window.

"Did you tell anyone about me before you died?" His voice was only a whisper, but it echoed in his soul with the fervor of a screaming crowd as the executioner raised his axe over a condemned man. "Have I not just begged God to have mercy on your soul? Give me some comfort! Tell me you died in silence!"

But there was no voice in the hushed chapel that gave him either solace or warning. His stomach churned. He begged and then begged again. "Do I not have the right to walk the earth in peace, if I do so meekly and ask only that I serve God?"

He wept.

The silence grew heavier.

Fithian staggered to his feet and raised his hands to the altar. "Did You not create me as I am? Have I not served You with greater devotion than many others with the right to take vows? And, until now, have you not let me?" He covered his eyes and wailed.

As he did, thin fingers reached out from the shadows

and gripped the back of the cord holding the cross around his neck.

They jerked it tight.

Fithian struggled, but only for a moment. As the darkness of eternity began to blind him, his last thought was that God was being kind. It was better to die like this and escape his inevitable earthly fate. After all, he was not dying by his own hand, and thus there was no sin in it.

20

The morning began with a scream of horror from a lay brother. It ended with the sad contemplation of another violent death.

Sister Anne rose from her knees. "Father Fithian was strangled with the strap holding his cross. That is the obvious cause of his murder, although we shall examine his body further."

Ralf carefully did not look at the prioress, who was leaning over the sub-infirmarian's shoulder during the examination. Nor would he voice his first thought that perhaps this death might have been prevented if he had been allowed to start the investigation immediately. His second thought was to admit he had no reason to believe there would have been any difference. The timing of the two deaths was too close. Yet he was impatient for Eleanor to take action and query her cousin. In his opinion, this unusual jousting over authority was petty. Getting on with catching the perpetrator ought to be primary.

"Lest anyone wonder, the priest could not have done this himself." The sub-infirmarian looked around at those waiting for her verdict. "Does anyone have a question?"

The two hospital lay brothers lowered their gaze and murmured prayers for the priest's soul.

Thomas frowned. "A man is the most likely killer?"

Shaking her head, Sister Anne replied, "I cannot say that with certainty, Brother. Father Fithian was thin and short. If he was caught by surprise and the murderer was swift, he would have quickly lost all awareness. A woman could have strangled him."

Thomas sighed. "Then we must know where everyone was..."

"After Compline, when he was seen at prayer with others, and before Prime when the corpse was discovered," Sister Anne said. "I shall soon ask where all the nuns and lay sisters were for this death as well."

"You found none of them who could not give a good account of themselves during the time the countess was killed." Eleanor realized that the only ones so far who could not provide a satisfactory alibi for the first murder were her cousin and the maid. Neither could Sister Serena, but the prioress was incapable of imagining that such a child would be a reasonable suspect. Yet the nun was also absent to complete her penance of prayer during the likely time of this killing. She shook her head and tried, unsuccessfully, to banish that uncomfortable fact from her thoughts.

"Why would the priest come to this chapel, of all places? He knew it was where the countess was killed." Brother Thomas instinctively looked around.

"I had forbidden him to leave his quarters for his own safety until I had summoned him," Eleanor said. "But I had not, yet I saw him earlier in the day talking to you, Brother. Was your meeting outside accidental, or did you invite him from his quarters to walk with you?"

"It was accidental, my lady." He thought for a moment

and then added, "After we briefly spoke, he said he must go to prayer. I believe the bells had rung for the Office."

Eleanor realized that he may have disobeyed her because he felt compelled to go with others to the church for prayer. If he was as rigorous in strict practices of faith as suggested, then he might well have done that. It was something she should have considered and insisted on sending a monk to accompany him. Yet he had not died because he went to a late Office with others. He had died because he had been in the chapel alone. Had someone he knew sent for him?

"Have you heard from Prior Vincent about where the men were during the time of the first murder?" Ralf hoped this task had been done, but he suspected otherwise.

"Brother Beorn interrogated the lay brothers," Eleanor said, "and all were at their assigned tasks. Prior Vincent still has a few monks to question."

The crowner bit his tongue. There were far more lay brothers at Tyndal than monks, yet this idiot of a prior was incapable of doing even this simple task? He could tell from Eleanor's tone that she was equally annoyed, so he chose not to rub the salt of his own disgust into the festering wound of her frustration.

Thomas concluded that it was unlikely that those previously questioned and found to be most probably innocent would be under suspicion for this crime either.

"Is the small storage room adjacent to this chapel adequate for your further examination, now that the body of my cousin's wife has been moved to the hospital?" When Sister Anne agreed, Eleanor ordered the two lay brothers to take the new corpse there.

Once the body was gone, Eleanor quickly examined the area, hoping for another clue like the one she had found with Eda. Near the altar, not far from where the body had lain, she saw a flash of light and leaned over to retrieve the object. It was a ring. Had it been there for some time, or had it been pulled from the killer's hand by Father Fithian in his struggle for air? She showed it to Ralf, Brother Thomas, and Sister Anne. None recognized it.

Ralf started to reach out for it but quickly pulled back his hand when the prioress slipped it into her pouch.

"It looks like a man's ring," Thomas said. "If it belonged to the one who killed the priest, then it is more likely a man committed both crimes, my lady." He thought for a moment. "If the ring has nothing to do with this crime, then we are still left with the possibility that a woman could have been the murderer if surprise was a factor."

"And passion gives strength to the arm dealing the blow, Brother," the sub-infirmarian replied. "Indeed, I wish I could discount a conclusion that a woman might have committed both crimes. It would eliminate many from consideration. We might not have a likely suspect, but we don't need to have double the number of people to question."

"And I know we all share the desire to resolve this as quickly as possible," Eleanor said with a quick look at the crowner. "While Sister Anne is completing her examination of this new corpse, I shall seek out my cousin for questioning. I will take the ring to see if he recognizes it and soon return it to you, Ralf."

Before anyone could respond, shrill screams came from the room where Father Fithian's body had been taken.

Both lay brothers ran toward the prioress, pale as bone and waving their hands.

"My lady! My lady! There is a devil in there!"

"Flee!" shouted the other. "Our souls are in danger!"

21

Brother Thomas put a hand on a shoulder of each lay brother. "Calm yourselves. This is God's place, and He will protect you." The monk had no doubt the men had seen something terrifying. Both shook as if suffering the force of a terrible gale, and one was standing in a puddle of his own urine.

The other man found his voice. "We did not imagine this. Satan has sent one of his vilest imps to attack us. The creature is in there. He revealed himself in all his unnatural foulness."

Eleanor knew this man as one disinclined to strange imaginings. Yet she also had no reason to think there was anything in that small room that should lead to such panic. When she first arrived, she had glanced in to make sure Eda's body had been removed and noticed nothing that should cause this reaction. "I shall go see..."

"Please, my lady! Do not. Even those as blessed as you are in grave danger from what lies there. It is beyond description. It is— I fear—I cannot—" He began to weep.

His companion grabbed him around the shoulders in an

attempt to comfort, but his eyes were filled with terror as well.

The sub-infirmarian went to the crowner and said, "Ralf, please take these men to the hospital. They need blankets for warmth and unwatered wine to drink. Tell Sister Oliva that they have been given a shock, and she will know what to do to heal the damage done."

"Do you not need me here?" He bent his head toward the room where the presumed imp waited for his next victim. Although he was not inclined to superstition, and doubted he had ever seen anything more evil than mortal man, he was sweating.

"Return as soon as possible, but Brother Thomas, Sister Anne, and I will investigate in the meantime," Eleanor said. "There was no devil there when we arrived, but a trio of monastics hold the power of the Trinity against anything untoward that may have ascended from Hell." She pointed to the altar. "Besides, this is a chapel devoted to God's worship. No imp can tolerate being too close to God for long enough to do us harm."

"Come with me," the crowner said to the two lay brothers. "I will accompany you back to the hospital."

"What if the thing follows us?" The face on this calmer lay brother had remained shock-white.

Ralf turned so his sword hilt was visible. "All soldiers know that this can serve as God's protection in times of need. Does it not look like a cross?" It was an argument he had used on many occasions. Raw troops found comfort in the symbolism as they faced the possibility of death in battle. The dying looked on it with hope when their fellow soldiers took their confessions as death began to cloud their vision.

The two lay brothers took in a deep breath and left with

a slight return of color that suggested great relief at their escape.

"And now we must see what is in that room," Eleanor said, and the trio walked toward the doorway.

The small space was utterly silent. There was no stench of evil. Even the body had yet to emit any whiff of death that would eventually surpass the unwashed reek of the priest while he lived.

They briefly checked the area but saw nothing that suggested an imp—or anything at all that might be interpreted as such.

The body of Father Fithian lay sprawled on the ground where he seemed to have been dropped.

Thomas knelt beside it.

"What could they have seen that made them disrespect a priest's body in this manner?" Sister Anne looked down in dismay. "They are both experienced in caring for the sick. There is little they have not seen, from terrible wounds to the agonizing decay of lepers at the end of their suffering."

Thomas studied the body for a long time without touching it. The priest lay with his face pressed against the stones of the floor. Once again, the monk was struck by the disparity between the man's unkempt body and the clean head with neatly trimmed tonsure. "I see only the wound caused by the strangling cord," he said, looking up at Sister Anne, who had come closer to view the corpse. Yet she still kept a chaste distance in accordance with the vows both she and the priest had taken.

The monk grasped the shoulders. "Strong," he remarked. "I wonder if he had once been a soldier." Yet, as the sub-infirmarian had remarked earlier, the priest was otherwise remarkably thin. Had he chosen to fast excessively? Thomas wondered.

He flipped the corpse over. The man's robe slipped farther up around his hips.

Thomas started. Was he imagining what he thought he saw?

His hand shaking, he reached out and carefully lifted the robe to look closer, then cried out in shock.

Father Fithian possessed both male and female genitals.

22

"He was a hermaphrodite," Sister Anne said.

Eleanor was stunned into silence.

"I have read about such an affliction, but I have never met anyone who suffered it." Thomas had quickly pulled the priest's robe down out of respect for the corpse, but he continued to gaze at the body as if he still could not believe what he had witnessed.

"I have. Once," the sub-infirmarian replied. "A woman came to me, begging for help because she feared she might be unable to bear a child. She longed to wed a man who wished the union too."

"I confess I wondered if Father Fithian was other than he presented himself, but my conversation with him was very brief and I did not ponder the doubts long," Thomas continued. "He spoke indistinctly, but the pitch of his voice did not suggest femininity. His shoulders were those of a man. His features offered no clue, although his lips were fuller than men usually have. Yet there was very little to suggest this." Thomas gestured at the body. "As for the lack of a beard, I assumed he did not have much and kept the little he grew closely shaven." He bent closer to the body. "And that may still have been the case. I cannot tell."

"I now understand why he did not bathe," Eleanor whispered with sorrow. "He could not chance discovery."

"Nor did I have cause to think the woman who came to me was different until I examined her," Sister Anne said.

"Was there any hope for her?" Eleanor blinked as if struggling with tears.

"Sadly not. I have since learned that hermaphrodites are either assigned a gender by their parents or choose one themselves later if none has been assigned. They are not prohibited from marriage if the prospective spouse is willing. Some assigned as women can have children. With the woman I knew, her womb was incomplete and bearing children was not possible. Even if the man she loved had been willing to ignore her very rudimentary male genitals, he could not accept her barrenness, as the Church might refuse to wed them. She had to turn him away."

"What happened to her?"

"She was found dead soon after. The man she loved loudly proclaimed that he was the one to reject her, although he gave no reason. Some claimed she had jumped off the cliff deliberately in despair over his rejection. Others said she had surely fallen accidentally. In the end, everyone decided it was an accident, and she was allowed burial in holy ground." The sub-infirmarian looked at her companions for a moment. "I was asked by a priest if I knew whether she had probably committed self-murder because she had come to me not long before her death. I said I did not, a truth because no one knows why anyone would choose Hell over hope. Since she had no family, I offered to wash her body myself and dress it in grave clothes. As far as I knew, her secret remained her own, and if her prospective spouse was aware, he said nothing. In any case, when one of their own has committed no offense against anyone, neighbors often choose mercy by doing what they can to allow Christian burial."

Eleanor touched her friend's shoulder, knowing she still grieved over this woman's death.

"I have heard no rumor about Father Fithian," Thomas said, "so I believe he was not generally known to be a hermaphrodite. Having been determined to be male, he could have become a priest and remained such. The only prohibition is that the choice, once made, is permanent. Had he once acted as a woman and that fact been discovered, he could not have remained a priest." Thomas blinked as something occurred to him, but he said nothing aloud.

As the two women considered his information, all fell silent.

Eleanor spoke first. "He has been murdered. Does this new revelation point to anyone who might have discovered his secret and had some reason to kill him for it? And how must we now approach the murder of my cousin's wife? Might the two killings be connected?"

"The two deaths might not be connected," Sister Anne said. "And Brother Thomas has mentioned a potentially significant detail. Perhaps we need to consider if he did change genders, and the consequences of that act are why someone killed him." Sister Anne bit her lip. "I do not know if I am forbidden to examine the body directly since he chose to be a man." She hesitated. "Brother, would you check to see if he has a woman's breasts or hips?"

"He has larger breasts than any man with his thinness," he said after touching the priest's chest. "I am unsure about the hips."

She asked him to pull the priest's robe closer to the body, then bent to look. "Narrow for a woman, but not unusual. Wide for a man? Perhaps." She looked at Thomas. "You had more contact with him. Might he have been accepted as a woman as well as a man?"

"I have heard other women speak in a similar pitch. He was not unusually short for a man nor too tall for a woman, especially if her ancestors settled here from the Viking lands." He closed his eyes as if visualizing the dead priest in more feminine attire. "His shoulders were too broad for most women, but I would have had little difficulty in accepting womanhood if he had come to me with a husband in hand."

"Then the sight of dual genitals is why our lay brothers thought he was some imp belonging to the Prince of Darkness?" Eleanor asked.

"Presumably," Sister Anne responded.

"They might well have been unaware of this third gender. The condition is rather uncommon," Thomas said. "I knew of it from my studies. And I was aware of what the Church said was allowed or not for those so born." He turned to the sub-infirmarian. "And you knew…"

"Apart from the one person who came to me, it is a condition discussed at some length in medical texts, current and ancient. My father was aware that only two genders are accepted, even though three exist. Thus, he once told me, the hermaphrodite must be assigned to a male or female life to emulate Adam and Eve."

"This is what the Church has decided," Thomas added.

"The secular world is not always so forgiving," Eleanor said. "Men are terrified of the different, perhaps because they fear they will be infected by it and are afraid of mockery or rejection."

Thomas did not reply. Despite his comment, he was not even sure about the Church. If God was perfect, he wondered, how could He create the imperfect? Or was the third gender actually perfect and the narrower definition of only two, demanded by mortals, the imperfect element? The debate was one churchmen continued to have. Even though He had made Man in His image, the creature was defined as flawed and sinful because of original sin. With hermaphrodites, the solution was to grant one of the two acceptable sexes to perfect the imperfect, but weren't these genders still imperfect? Thomas's head began to hurt.

The two women were talking and did not see him wince with pain.

To add to his confusion, Thomas added a question he had never heard addressed. Was he born a hermaphrodite himself, albeit one heretofore undefined by either the ancient physicians and scholars or the ones today? He had no feminine physical attributes, but he did love men as a woman might. Yet he also longed to lie with men as a man does a woman. Must he define himself as strictly male or female too? And how could he do that? To choose to be a man might be logical from his appearance, but his heart still loved...

Thomas wanted to cry in frustration and pain. These two murders were not only tragic in themselves but had presented him with more questions to ask God. Just when he felt he was beginning to come to terms with Him, he was faced with further complications. How much more could he bear?

He rose to his feet and went to stand by the door alone.

As she looked down on the body of the dead man, Eleanor also had questions without answers. How could God form a man who was also a woman or a woman who was also a man? Had the woman who came to Sister Anne committed any sin, before her self-murder, except that of birth? It was true that the Church would not condemn her as long as she lived the life of one gender and never changed. How could Father Fithian have offended?

Although he had become a priest in defiance of secular fears, the Church had accepted him. Yet had his mixed gender brought about his death, a violence unconnected to the stabbing of Eda, or was it connected in some still-hidden way?

Eleanor never liked the complicated in investigating murders. The reasons for the crimes might be involved, but she did not think killers committing multiple murders were usual outside, perhaps, London. And certainly sequential murders inside a walled priory were even rarer. The potential guilty one could be anyone here, she thought sadly, then with grim humor reminded herself that there was least one innocent in the priest's death. Eleanor did not believe in lethal ghosts, and therefore someone other than the dead countess was the perpetrator.

Two killers? Of course that was possible, although she was usually inclined to dismiss that complication too. Other than in mobs or battle, men usually killed for personal reasons. Maybe the powerful employed experts to murder rivals. King Edward had almost died in the Holy Land at the hand of an assassin in the hire of Sultan Baibars. But her cousin's wife? A common priest? These did not have the marks of crimes committed for the sake of power or fame.

She clenched her teeth. Enough was enough. She must hesitate no longer in confronting her cousin. Ralf would be right to take over the investigation if she delayed further. Were the situation reversed, she certainly would do so.

"I must see my cousin," Eleanor said to Anne. "This second murder demands it." Then she added, "I may have to reveal what we have just learned here to him, but he will not speak of it if I ask him not to do so."

Sister Anne nodded. "Go, for you have no further worries here. I have just sent for two of my most trusted lay brothers to take the corpse to the hospital." The sub-infirmarian looked at the pensive monk. "Would you prepare the body for burial, Brother? I will help as our vows permit, but I can only trust you in this. We dare not have morbid rumors of imps and spirits circulating like fog through the priory."

He agreed, and his expression even suggested he was glad she had asked him to do this.

"You have always been my support and confident," Eleanor replied in a loving voice to the sub-infirmarian. "One thing more, since it will be several hours yet before I can visit her chambers. How is Sister Ruth?"

Sister Anne brightened. "She is regaining strength! The apoplectic attack may have been far less severe than feared. She is awake, although she has weakness in her left arm, and her speech is not as clear as it once was." The nun looked skyward with honest gratitude. "I will see her soon, let her know of your concern, and promise that you will come to her shortly." She smiled briefly. "Sister Christina remains by her side for hours, and her prayers have been of supreme comfort to our former sub-prioress."

Eleanor nodded with relief. Sister Christina, the hospital infirmarian, was widely regarded to be on her way to sainthood. Not only was her kindness a healing cure for much of human pain, but her prayers were noted for their efficacy. It was also Sister Christina who stood up to the suspicions many felt for what they deemed questionable treatments by Sister Anne. When this venerated nun proclaimed that God had directly inspired her sub-infirmarian with holy wisdom, most critics fell silent. When Tyndal's hospital became famous for its cures and those of high rank came for healing, only the most irrational continued to object.

"And I shall visit soon. Now I must go to my cousin."

"You must take someone with you."

"I cannot. My cousin may tell me things he would not if a stranger is there."

"If he is the killer..."

Eleanor bit her cheek to keep from an instant, ill-considered response. She did not believe David was a killer, especially of women. Many men who were fearless warriors were as gentle as fawns when the heat of battle was over. Even if he had hated his wife, he would not have killed her and most certainly not in the chapel of Tyndal Priory. As for the relationship with her cousin, she and David had a deep bond that dated back as far as she could recall. This meant she might lack needed objectivity, but it could also mean she was in an excellent position to judge whether he could be a murderer. Nonetheless, she understood why Sister Anne was concerned, and, as objective as Eleanor believed herself to be, she also knew that her friend had rational cause.

"I will take someone with me, but he may not enter the room itself where I will meet with my cousin—or listen in. If there is any threat, I promise to call out for aid. It will be safe enough, for I will leave the door open."

The expression on Sister Anne's face clearly revealed her doubts. But she nodded out of respect and the knowledge that her friend rarely put herself in danger when she could avoid it. Other than a broken arm and a bump on the head, Eleanor had caught many murderers with little physical damage, although more than a few threats. Sister Anne reached out and gently touched Eleanor's arm. "God be with you," she murmured.

Eleanor left to find the Earl of Ness.

23

Eleanor waited for her cousin to return to his quarters and greet her. A lay brother had been left standing near the door in case of need, although she had no doubt that his vigil was unnecessary. Meanwhile, she took out the ring and studied it.

Normally, she would have been delighted to find clues left behind for each of the two murders, but she felt uneasy about the cross and ring. The former was light and loose in form. The loss might have been explained by assuming the murderer had not noticed the absence until it was too late to retrieve it. But a ring was more easily felt as it was pulled off and then rolled some distance away from the body. Would it have logically rolled to the place where she found it? And wouldn't a quick search have revealed it? It hadn't taken her long to see it, and she hadn't been focused on finding a lost ring.

The clues might well have been deliberately left.

She always allowed for many possibilities in each new murder she had to solve, but she usually discounted most early on. In this case, she had to consider two contradictory conclusions, both of which held the strong likelihood of being true. The first was two-pronged: that the clues were true ones or else lost accidentally. The necklace suggested a woman, while the ring pointed to a man. Yet the ring might have been lost by anyone who had come here innocently to pray—and so could the necklace. But the second was that the clues had been intended to deceive, and that meant the murderer had a motive in leaving each. If so, what was the intended misdirection, and how might the solution to that question lead one to the right one?

"You wished to see me, Cousin?"

Eleanor was startled but managed to hide the ring in her fist. Recovering, she replied with a gentle smile. "You know why I am here. We must talk. I need your help."

David's eyes narrowed. "I have said all I have to impart. Your monk can confirm my mood, what I said, how I searched this room..."

"There has been a second death."

The earl sat down with a thud on the edge of the storage box at the end of his bed and stared. "A second?" His expression was sick with horror.

"Father Fithian." She saw no reason to hide or soften the news.

"That is impossible!"

"Why?"

He threw up his hands with a hint of annoyance. "Fithian reeked like a cart of night soil, but he was a quiet, pious soul. I liked him. We spoke often of spiritual matters when I could sit upwind from him. He had no enemies. Are you sure this was murder?"

"He was strangled."

David covered his eyes with a hand. "May God forgive what few sins the man could have owned. I shall pay for prayers on his behalf."

"What do you know of Father Fithian's past? Both you

and he were in the Holy Land at the same time. I need to learn as much as possible. He was killed for some reason. Do not set aside anything, no matter how trivial."

"I understand what you need, dear Cousin. I assure you that I want to help, but I swear I have little enough to tell you."

"Anything. Please." Eleanor gestured for him to begin.

Looking up at her with sorrow, he began. "I know nothing of where he was born or about his family. I met him in the Holy Land when he was a priest in the household of a brother crusader. According to what the latter told me, Father Fithian had saved his life. I never asked if this was in battle or because of some plot discovered by the priest, nor do I know anyone still alive who might. In any case, the crusader told me he had promised the priest a permanent livelihood because of what he had done for him." He stood up and looked around, quickly spying a jug of wine. He offered some to Eleanor and then poured a mazer for them both.

Sipping her drink, Eleanor quietly waited for her cousin to sit down again.

"That crusader died of a fever, and my wife's brother offered to take Father Fithian into his household. I assume this had been prearranged, but I cannot confirm it. When he decided to return home, Father Fithian went with him. I saw them off on the ship. I did not return myself until after my wife's brother had been killed. Murdered. The one who did it was never found. The priest was then accepted into my wife's household, where he remained. She claimed to me that she needed a confessor. These are facts I know. Anything else is hearsay."

"What else did you hear and from whom? I acknowledge the problems with rumor, but I must know what was said as accurately as you can recall the words."

He paused. "This next likely means nothing, but you said to tell you any detail."

She eagerly nodded.

"The sources are varied. Some men I had known in the Holy Land. Not well, but crusaders have a unique kinship. A few said they had overheard servants talking. But the basic tale was the same from all. It seems the priest felt a fiercer loyalty to the first man he served than most of us realized. Father Fithian wept like a widow over the death of this man and barricaded himself in the chapel. He refused to eat and only emerged when another priest told him that he was committing self-murder if he continued. Do you need to know the names of those who told me?"

"Not yet. The tale is enough since so many told the same one. I will ask only if I need the information." She thought for a moment. "Did the priest change any afterward?"

"No stories about that came to my ears. Since there were none, I assumed Father Fithian found solace for his deep sorrow. He had always been pious. Perhaps he was more reclusive, but I knew him better when he served my wife, not before in the Holy Land."

"What more do you know?"

"Little enough. Father Fithian had become confessor to my wife by the time I came home. She told me that her former priest had died and she knew Father Fithian was well respected by those in his old household. Others might have taken him in, but only she had an immediate need for a confessor, so she was happy to do as her brother had once asked."

How convenient, Eleanor thought, that a position was available for him at just the right time so Eda could honor her brother's request. Was this important? "You approved?"

He laughed. "I had no reason to care. As it soon became evident after my arrival home, my wife had come to loathe my body and my bed during my absence. Not that she had ever enjoyed paying the marital debt, but she had pretended often enough to quicken with our still-living children as well as a few dead ones. Just a few days after I stepped off the boat, she told me that only piety could be her lover as well as her soul's salvation. After that, she and I led very separate lives. I did not care what she did as long as it did not bring disgrace on our family."

Eleanor raised a questioning eyebrow.

"I had no cause to blame Father Fithian for this, Cousin. I asked him bluntly enough. He said it was his belief that a husband and wife should enjoy each other. Since her desire to reject me was based in faith, however, the decision was hers. She had queried him on whether she had the right to deny me because she longed for celibacy. He had tried to argue against this, but she was determined. We had enough children, she told him, and she wanted to take a vow of abstinence. The Church was on her side."

"You willingly took up a separate household?"

"To be honest, I did not like our couplings either. In her youth, she had a bonny enough body, but she was always sour in nature. Because of the vows we took, I wanted to be faithful to her, and children were needed, but I had no reason to grieve over her decision. I travel alone to visit friends, property, and kings. She stays in our castle in Scotland where she secludes herself with her collection of crosses and lives in front of an altar. Occasionally, she invites the local bishop when she longs for profound discussions about sin." He hesitated, as if rethinking what he was about to say.

Eleanor caught that. "Say it, Cousin."

"Even as a small girl, you never joined others in telling tales or spreading rumors." He briefly grinned at her. "But you listened closely enough anyway, and your friends found you owned a gentle ear. I am not surprised you became so skilled at hunting down miscreants."

"If you fear your thoughts will be revealed, I swear to forget them as long as they are irrelevant to these crimes or can be replaced with other facts."

"It is less that than the remark which just came to mind. It will sound rude, but I mean no ill. What I was about to say was that if Eda had been born male, she might have become such an ardent priest that angels would feel sinful in comparison. I also noticed that our local bishop always gave inspired sermons after one of his discussions with my wife. He loved to name the wicked and bring down public shame on those who thought their sins were hidden."

"Then you suspect that the source of his knowledge might have been your wife—or even Father Fithian?"

"More likely my wife! As for Fithian, I never saw any hint of the zealot in him. I doubt he cared much for the falsities, games, and fantasies of worldly men. He spent more time on his knees than most, yet he never spoke of his piety. My wife concluded he was especially holy because he never bathed." He shot Eleanor an impish smile. "I will say, for the comfort of her ladies, it was well my wife did not choose to follow that one example of his holiness she seemed most to admire."

"Did Fithian have any secrets, rumored or known, other than his strong reaction to the death of the man he served?"

"Silence about family and his past suggest two things to me. He was either someone with something to hide or a man who longed to reject the world and never again wanted to speak about what he had cast aside."

Eleanor decided to tell her cousin the truth and watch his reaction. "Did you know that Father Fithian was a hermaphrodite?"

David's jaw dropped. "A lie! Surely! Where did you hear that?"

"It is no lie, Cousin. We discovered it when his corpse was examined after his death. Did anyone else know?"

The earl gasped for breath. For a long time, all he could do was shake his head. Finally, he said, "Had it been known, I surely would have heard. Nor did my wife know. She would have had him flung out of the house to freeze to death on the king's road." He stopped, then murmured, "Must this become known?"

Either her cousin wanted to hide the shocking secret to protect the reputations of his family and household or he respected what he had known of the priest enough not to want his memory tainted with scurrilous tales. Knowing him, she suspected the latter. "It shall remain a secret. Sister Anne has arranged for his body to be prepared for burial by Brother Thomas."

"Will you bury him here? Please?"

That might require some research, Eleanor thought. But Brother Thomas would know the answer to that. He had, after all, studied canon law. And he did say the Church would have condoned the calling of one deemed a man to the priesthood. God is merciful, she thought. The woman of whom Sister Anne had spoken was also buried in holy soil.

She agreed to her cousin's plea, and, when asked, he vowed never to mention what he had just learned.

Now she had one more thing to discuss with her cousin. How ought she to handle it? Being coy was rarely her chosen approach. Nor had she ever been less than forthright with the Earl of Ness. She opted for the straightforward and opened her hand to reveal the ring. "Have you ever seen this?" She stretched out her hand for him to see and touch the object.

He stiffened and glared at it, but his answer came swiftly

enough. "Yes. That belongs to a friend of mine at court. He told me he had lost it and was deeply grieved because it was a gift from King Edward."

"Not yours?"

He showed her his hands. He wore one ring with a worn band and a glittering ruby. "The only ring I wear is this one my father bequeathed me on his death bed. Other than in my vain youth, have you ever seen another ring on my hand?"

Thinking back to David before his marriage, she remembered how much he liked to glitter and shine with gold, jewels, and fashionable dress to attract young women. After his marriage, and especially after his time as a crusader, he turned to plainer attire and little adornment, as befitted a graver man. Not austere exactly, but hardly ostentatious.

"No, I have not."

"Where was it found?"

"Near the body of the priest."

"Thus your crowner might well ask why this ring, belonging to my friend at court, would be found on your chapel floor. And why was my knife the weapon that killed my wife? Cousin, I know suspicion is turned my way, but I swear to you that I did not kill my wife and had no reason to kill the priest."

She believed him—or at least her woman's heart did. But did her more masculine reason? At this moment, she simply did not know. The heart's defense drowned out whatever cautions the mind might be whispering to her. She would have to deal with their debate in the silence of her own chambers, when she could listen impartially.

Suddenly, he raised his hand and smiled. "At least I may have a witness to my innocence in Father Fithian's murder! Last night, I could not sleep and decided to take a walk to the stables. I have no doubt that your lay brothers care well for the horses, but mine is special to me. He and I have ridden together for a long time. I have found him to be a patient listener." His look betrayed a deep affection for the creature.

Eleanor might well understand the nature of talks between man and horse. After all, did she not have discussions of profound matters with her cat? Yet she was not about to let him take this more pleasant side path away from the rougher road to truth she was determined they follow.

But David had no more intention of delay than she and quickly continued. "As I hurried to the stable, I saw a man passing whom I have since learned was your prior. He might have noticed me and could confirm my story. It must have been just after the bells had rung for prayer. I cannot be sure because I had been lost in thought about other matters and did not notice the tolling. But he was certainly in a hurry to pray and could confirm both time and whether he saw me."

"That would indeed help, Cousin!" Eleanor rose and told David that she might have more questions later, but the next Office would soon demand her own presence in prayer. She did not ask if he would join her. His faith had been proven by observing his vows to go to the Holy Land to recover Jerusalem. How he chose to honor God after that was a matter between him and his priest.

As she left, she still felt uneasy. Was her cousin telling her everything? If he and his wife had separated, might David not have formed some attachment to another woman? Many men might be content enough with maids and occasional ladies at court. Her elder brother fancied married women, with whom he had brief and cordial affairs. But David was like his mother who had given her whole heart only once and, when her husband died, had taken vows at Amesbury. Had David found a woman to give his

137

heart to that once in a lifetime after the chill of his marriage? If so, might it be significant in the murder of his wife? Might the priest have seen David at the wrong time, just as he claimed Prior Vincent had seen him at the right time? That would explain why her cousin might have killed both his wife and the priest.

She shook her head in annoyance. She still had questions for Jennet, who was lying to her as well as her cousin. And, to be fair, Sister Serena needed to be questioned. She claimed to have spent all night in solitary prayer, but had she? Had her confessed terror of the world been sparked into violence by something that happened with either Eda or Father Fithian? Eleanor felt this might be too far-fetched, but her knowledge of the nun's past was meager, and there was too much oddity in this duet of deaths already.

24

Thomas failed to see even a hint of morning light in the east, but winter was an ally of the Prince of Darkness. God might ultimately rule the earth, he thought as he made his way toward the anchoress's window, but His formerly loved angel was a stubborn adversary. These months were aptly named the Dark Season in Satan's honor.

The Anchoress Juliana slept so little that he wondered how she always managed to greet the suffering with such kindness and wisdom or even how she survived. Thomas could do without rest on occasion, but his wits dimmed after too little of it. Yet she knew that some must come to her during Satan's hours because they could no longer endure life without her soothing counsel. To get it, they were willing to chance the survival of their souls against the Devil's vilest plots, which were best created and executed when no light could destroy them. Thomas knew he would not be the only mortal she had dragged back from the sin of self-murder.

He wanted to weep, not because of his own torments, but because of what Father Fithian must have suffered.

Thomas was allowed the company of the man he loved, albeit under tragic circumstances. Had the priest enjoyed even a moment of joy with the one he had loved?

He grieved for the priest and offered a prayer for his soul. When Thomas had undressed Father Fithian to bathe his body for burial, he was prepared for the sight of a body with feminine breasts and the residual genitalia of both genders. But he was perplexed by the cloth bag Fithian had worn under his robe and which rested near his heart.

As he had removed the robe, Thomas pulled the bag over the priest's head and turned to set it aside as well. But he was curious and opened it. Inside, there was a folded and well-worn piece of dark cloth with a white cross. When he pulled it out, an arrowhead stained with faint traces of blood along with a bent cross fell out.

Others might have wondered what this meant. Thomas did not. Whatever the full tale was, he knew that Father Fithian had loved the crusader whose life he once saved and kept these items as the only things remaining to give him comfort after his beloved had died. In sleep or prayer or his duties as a priest, Fithian always had something next to his heart to comfort him.

After he washed the priest's body, he slipped the bag around the man's neck again and then dressed the corpse in its shroud for burial. He decided Fithian could sleep until Judgment Day with the comfort he needed to rest in peace. It was up to God to then decide whether the man's love was worthy of eternal mercy.

When Thomas arrived at his usual spot behind the bush, he saw no shadow leaning against the curtained window of the anchoress. With gratitude, Thomas hurried to it and eased himself to his knees. Had another suppliant been there, he would have left.

Briefly, he gazed into the darkness, chose a faint star in the sky on which to focus, and sighed a word of thanks to God for this gift of succor he was about to receive.

"Brother Thomas." The voice from within was deep and melodic.

"Aye." He could not see her, but she always knew when he knelt here and her greeting was invariably warm. "I have come for guidance from you."

"Not from me," she said softly. "You are a priest and Adam's son. I am a wicked daughter of Eve. God has chosen to bless this anchorage and often uses my tongue to convey His wisdom and wishes. He understands that His voice may be needed when priests sleep, for men often long to find comfort when the Prince of Darkness attacks their souls in the silence of the night."

Thomas felt a little calm slip into him with those words. "I, most certainly, have problems with that silence, and prayers set by the Church never seem meant for creatures such as I to utter."

"I think you understand God better than most, Brother, even when you believe otherwise. Where you struggle most seems to be in accepting that He loves you."

Her pitch had dropped deeper. He knew this meant she had changed from the woman known as Juliana into God's channel.

"It is Durant, is it not?"

Had he not known that she remained behind the curtain and the thick stone wall that formed the border of the window, he would have sworn she was whispering in his ear. He did not bother to speak. She knew what he was thinking without his speech.

"The wine merchant has asked that you help cleanse

him of his sins and lead him to God. You believe you are unworthy of this task and might endanger his path because of your own sins. We have spoken of this before."

"I have accepted this duty as my penance, yet I continue to be struck with irritation, blindness, and new reasons to doubt my ability. Durant may think he needs me to help him understand his own feelings for, say, his wife, because they are contradicted by his..." Thomas stopped and held his breath. He did not continue since he could not put adequate words to his thoughts. Instead, he said, "I fear his concerns and doubts are little different from my own. How can I guide him if I am as ignorant of the answers as he?"

"Why did our beloved hermit of Tyndal give you this penance? I do not mean to ask what sin you had committed but rather what lesson were you supposed to learn from it?"

"Love."

"Then you have, within yourself, the answer to your question, Brother. God is perfection, and God is love. That means that love has many manifestations but the total is perfection, something men can only approximate. Let me address that approximation. Durant, for instance, profoundly loves his wife, his children, and one other."

Thomas suddenly felt naked, then realized it was his soul that had been stripped and not his body.

"All are different forms of love. He lay with his wife, perhaps with lust or maybe only with the semblance of it, and children came into the world. As his vowed life companion and mother of those children, his wife owns a treasured part of his heart." She drew in a deep breath. "The love he bears his children is not at issue here."

"No," he murmured.

"He sinned much over many years in ways the Church condemns with great vigor. He believes he has been punished for that with a lingering death and great pain."

142

"He said it drove him to retire to Tyndal and seek God's forgiveness."

"And to seek the comfort for the rest of his days that only you can bring him?"

Said this way, Thomas felt as if a boulder had been lifted from his back. He nodded and clung to this relief he feared would soon vanish.

"Master Durant loves his wife, as I have said. Yet he has chosen to leave her and retire here. That may hurt and trouble her deeply. Know that, yet understand that he has chosen to die in your arms, not hers."

How wicked he was, Thomas thought. Had he been Megge, he would have felt anger, hatred, and betrayal. Yet he had only observed sadness in her. "She is a good woman and deserves no pain," he said.

"Let her know that her husband loves her as he has always done, for I believe that to be true. Perhaps she found their marriage practices and routines a joy for her own reasons. If so, she needs confirmation that their love remains as strong as it has always been. Or she may be confused, hurt, and cannot grasp why he has left her. You will know best which is true if you allow your vision to clear and see with a kind heart. You are the chosen one, Brother. It is up to you to show the compassion required."

Thomas knew the audience was over. Juliana's voice had shifted back into the one that she alone owned.

"I hope whatever you heard was of help," she said.

Did she ever know what she said when God used her tongue? Thomas thanked her and left the window.

The darkness had begun its inevitable surrender, and a soft light was finally visible in the east. Now he could see a shape near the shrub he usually waited behind and opted to walk another way, toward the hospital and not back to the monks' dormitory.

143

As for his confusion and grief, he felt some easing. He and Durant shared a special love, a bonding the wine merchant had never had with Megge. She was his wife, but that was as the Church and men demanded of those not called to serve God. She had shared his bed on rare occasion. That was something Thomas would never enjoy with Durant. But, he said to himself, the anchoress had reminded him that it was with him that the wine merchant had chosen to end his time on earth and begin his journey to Heaven. That was the ultimate blessing and gift of love.

As the light grew stronger, Thomas knew he hadn't conquered all his fear and sadness, but he believed he had been given directions in how to do so with greater kindness and grace than he had felt before.

His additional questions for God could be set aside for the time being.

25

Although Eleanor required adherence to the Benedictine diet for the healthy religious that banished meat from any four-legged creatures, she did not follow the common monastic practice of only one daily meal in winter. Sister Anne believed some food was advisable to break the night fast, so Eleanor had ordered an obligatory serving of black bread and hard cheese to be eaten after the morning Office and before the day's work began. In accordance with the rules allowing small amounts of extra nourishment, she called this their pittance.

Her rank also allowed her a separate table in the refectory or to eat in the privacy of her quarters with prominent guests if she so wished. This morning, despite the visit of her cousin, she had chosen to eat with her nuns and lay sisters, and in the silence required at meals, she pondered what might be read during supper before the light vanished. It was necessary to choose a short passage to avoid any need to light candles. Perhaps something from Hildegard of Bingen? In an Order that reminded women of the influence and example of the Queen of Heaven, she believed it important that her nuns hear the wisdom of holy women.

After the morning pittance was over, Sister Gracia stopped her briefly to beg some time later to ask questions about the reading last evening. It was a time together they both cherished, and Eleanor refused to let even murder interfere with that.

When she finally returned to her chambers, Eleanor saw Sister Serena standing just outside the door.

What a sad child, she thought, yet she would be remiss if she did not question the nun on where she had been when the priest was killed. "Is your penance served?"

"It is, my lady, but I remain a wicked creature and fear that I shall sin again." When the nun raised her head, her face was as gray as the outside sky, her eyes were unfocused, and she began to tilt dangerously to one side.

Eleanor suddenly realized that she had not seen the nun at the pittance serving. She immediately took her by the arm and supported her into the audience chamber. Too much fasting, she concluded, and pushed the young woman down on the bench. "Sit," she said in a tone that few would dare contradict. In another instant, she had placed a hunk of old cheese and a torn piece of day-old bread beside her servant. "Eat it. Slowly. It is wicked to waste food."

Sister Serena studied the offering with the caution one might view a snake, glanced at her stern-faced mistress, and bit into the cheese.

She has sharp teeth, Eleanor noted as she watched the girl nibble with determined obedience and guilty hunger.

"The bread," Eleanor reminded her when the nun hesitated in chewing the rest of her obligatory meal. After Sister Serena had eaten as much as her sadly diminished stomach would allow, Eleanor indicated that she remain seated. "I must ask you some questions."

The girl silently bowed her head.

"Where did you spend your penitential time?"

"In the small chapel just below your chambers and apart from the main area of worship, my lady. I cannot tell you how long I was on my knees. As soon as I had gained your permission, I went there and did not leave until daybreak today. I came back here, but you had left your chambers."

"No one joined you in the chapel?"

"If anyone else came to pray, I did not notice. I chose a place not many would look and hoped I would be ignored. Man is such a vile beast. So many of us should spend more time alone and begging God's forgiveness for how badly we have corrupted His creation of mankind."

"You heard nothing?"

She shook her head. "God was kind, my lady. He lifted my soul up, let it sit in the palm of His hand, and allowed it to weep with remorse. He did not bless me with His speech, but I felt much comfort when my allotted time was done. It was as if I had been in a deep sleep and then had awakened from a lovely dream. Only at that moment did I hear the wind howling in the chapel and feel the chill of the dark night on my body."

"Then I must tell you that we have had another death in the priory. Father Fithian has been murdered."

Gasping with horror, the nun first hugged herself and then began to weep with terrible gulping sobs.

Eleanor sat beside her and hugged the gaunt body close until the sobbing calmed to mere gasps for breath.

"A holy priest? Slaughtered by some Devil's minion? In our sacred priory? Has my wickedness so tainted this place? My lady, might the Apocalypse be nigh as well?"

"What have you done that makes you think your deeds have been so terrible?" Eleanor hated asking the question.

147

The child was clearly grieving, and if the girl she held had been Gracia, she would have soothed, not interrogated.

"I was clumsy. I spilled the wine. I have been a dreadful servant to you. I do not know how to obey your simple commands..." She began to sob again.

"Nothing more than that?"

The nun shook her head but wept louder.

"Oh, hush, child! You have done nothing sinful. We all fail those we serve. Sometimes that is how we best learn wisdom, obedience, and humility." Sighing, she rocked the girl like a mother would her own child. "I may seem gruff. A prioress has many duties, and I often lack patience. But never fear to ask direction. I grieve if I have hurt you when you seek help. It is my sinful nature, and I apologize."

The nun pulled back and gazed up at Eleanor with a look of adoration. "You cannot err, my lady. You have been granted a vision of the Holy Family! God blessed you with that for your goodness."

"Do not speak of that event," Eleanor replied. "I am a frail creature like all of Eve's daughters. And I sin. We all do. But the greater sin is in not confessing our errors, begging forgiveness, and demanding penance." She looked down and smiled. "Always tell me the truth and do not fear consequences. I swear to stand by your side if any punishment is due and will try not to snap like a peevish dog as often as I have."

Eleanor truly meant this, but she also had another motive. Sister Serena might be a child to her mind, and an awkward one at that, but she also had no alibi for the time of the priest's death. As much as her heart wished she did not have to do this, her mind demanded she ask the question. "Have you told me the truth about what happened while you were performing your penance?"

"Of course! Would I endanger my soul further by saying

God had given me comfort if that was a lie? I still fear I am bound for Hell. My only hope is that God will see that my soul begs to be cleansed despite my reeking earthly shell."

"I only meant to ask if there was anyone with you or if you saw or heard anything outside the dream that God brought to comfort you."

Sister Serena again shook her head.

Eleanor hugged her and kissed the top of the girl's head. "Then be at peace. The evil that has invaded our priory has nothing to do with you. Brother Thomas and I are seeking out the cause as God demands. In the meantime, find the lay sister who has been your companion of late and go to Jennet, the woman who served the Countess of Ness. She should be in the chambers she shared with her dead mistress. When you find her, bring her here, for I must speak with her. Then, child, you will go into my private chambers and sleep on my bed."

"My lady, I cannot..."

Eleanor shook a finger at her. "That is an order, Sister."

With an eagerness that Eleanor found both touching and sad, Sister Serena leapt up and rushed to obey.

26

Jennet's demeanor as she entered the prioress's audience room suggested she anticipated a beating. Eleanor felt sorry for the maid and wondered how often her fears had been realized despite her insistence that Eda was kind. Jennet was so unskilled at deception that it did not take much for Eleanor to be convinced the woman had chosen to keep secret important information needed to clarify motive in this crime, or that she even knew the identity of the perpetrator. Yet she did not believe the maid had killed either mistress or priest. Never once had she known a mouse to kill a cat, and Jennet reminded her of a tiny rodent in a world of very large felines.

Although Eleanor longed to be gentle, she knew she dared not if she wanted to extract the truth. Perhaps because none of the initial suspects exhibited cruelty, greed, ambition or other characteristics common to violence, she was finding it especially difficult to be hard of heart with these inquiries. It made her unhappy, but she willed herself to the task.

She did not give the maid permission to sit in her presence, although she looked deeply weary. To do so might have allowed the woman to think she had earned a privilege and would pay no penalty for lying to a person of high rank.

"What do you know about Father Fithian?" she asked.

"Little enough, my lady. I confessed my sins to him, as did all those who served our mistress. My master had his own priest. His men went to that man to seek God's mercy."

An easy question for the maid, Eleanor decided as she noted how comfortable Jennet was answering it.

"Was he kind in his penances? Did he counsel you wisely or take time to explain where you had erred? You may tell me the truth. The details are important if I am to perform my own duty to God."

The maid considered the questions. "He was a quiet man. When not praying himself, he spent most of his time with our mistress, who seemed to have many things she longed to discuss. I would not say he assigned comfortable penances for sins, as some priests are inclined to order, nor did he delight in penitential cruelty as others do. Fasting was a common penance. Lengthy prayers when we were not required by our mistress were another. He never wanted to let a penance interfere with our earthly duties to those we served." She looked away and murmured, "I tried to perform them instead of getting more sleep."

A cleric well trained in the needs of noble households, Eleanor concluded. Yet he seemed to understand that mortals needed to show God sorrow for sinning while not gaining any perverse pleasure himself in making a fellow creature suffer more than needed. A man of moderation, it seemed.

"Quiet, you say?"

"He was most often found in the chapel, my lady. I must admit that none of us sought him out more than we were obliged to do and not because we didn't like or honor him. He may have been a virtuous man, but he did stink."

"Your mistress had no complaint about this?" Eleanor still found this hard to believe.

"She claimed it proved he was a holy man like the desert fathers."

"His stink, however, was no reason to kill him." Eleanor forced a smile. "Did he have enemies? Did he honor the sanctity of confession? Had he perhaps discovered some secret that a man or woman feared he might reveal?" Eleanor saw Jennet start when she mentioned that. Perhaps it was an issue she should pursue? She stopped and waited with an expression she hoped suggested that she knew the maid had something to say.

"I know of no enemies, my lady, and I never heard any rumor that he had ever revealed anything from confessions. As I said, we all believed him to be a quiet, fair, and pious priest."

And so she carefully avoids answering my last question, Eleanor decided with disgust. She was certain there was something hidden behind that wide-eyed gaze. After waiting a bit longer, she knew the maid would not willingly add anything more. Instead of pushing her, the prioress pulled the ring out of her pouch and passed it to Jennet.

"Do you recognize this?"

The maid turned chalk-white, yet she responded without hesitation. "I have seen one much like it on my master's hand." She shook her head. "Yet I do not want to mislead anyone. My memory may be faulty. It may not be my master's ring at all, but only like one I have often seen on his finger. The ruby is in the same place."

Her cousin had denied it was his, but Eleanor now knew with sadness that she had been right to refuse accepting his word without confirmation. "Does the earl wear many rings?"

Jennet shook her head. "Neither he nor my mistress wear much jewelry compared to others of their rank. She out of piety, although her collection of crosses was large and included fine gold and many gems. My master?" She blinked. "I do think I have seen this on his finger, but I cannot swear that it is different from the one he usually wears and beg you not to take my words as meaningful." She now stared at the object before returning it to the prioress. "It is a lovely thing, is it not? That red gem does glow even in this meager light." Wistfully, she added, "I once heard a tale about a knight who wore such a gem as a declaration of his heart's unending devotion to his lady."

"Do you recall if you might have seen it in Scotland or while he was here to attend the king?" Eleanor wasn't quite sure what difference it made, but if David did not wear it in Scotland, then there might be a significance in doing so at court.

"In Scotland, I believe. I cannot say he did not wear it at court, but I would only have been there with my mistress, not when he was with the king by himself."

That did not help, Eleanor thought, and put the ring back in her pouch. "You do not think it might be a woman's ring?"

"It is too big for anyone except a Viking queen, my lady. I have heard they are as big as their men and even go into battle."

Eleanor smiled at the reference and sat back. She had learned nothing useful that she had not already known. But she was aware that she had reason to think the maid might be in danger herself. Without knowing why the two victims had been killed, she could not discount a third murder.

"With all these deaths, child, you must be frightened by yourself."

"I am, my lady!"

Eleanor was taken aback by the terror she saw in Jennet's face. Was this what she had misconstrued as holding back a secret? Had she been too oblivious to the young woman's real fears? "Have you had cause to think you are in danger?"

"I think someone is watching me, even when I go to a more public chapel to pray. If I see a nun or lay sister, I beg for company on my way to meals. Once, when I returned, I thought someone might have been in the room I shared with my mistress. An item or two seemed out of place from what I remembered, and I know exactly what little I have moved." She stopped suddenly in this flood of words to think. "And I am sure the changes occurred later than your search of the room after her death."

"Have you noticed a particular person or something that might identify who this might be?"

"No, my lady, but I swear I am not seeing shadows where there are none."

Yet many would come to that conclusion, Eleanor thought, or else use the excuse to cast any questions about guilt away from themselves. No matter how reasonable the suspicion might be that Jennet was creating imps where there were none, Eleanor would not set aside the maid's words because they might be meaningless. That was neither compassionate nor wise.

"Then I shall arrange for you to stay in a more protected place," she said. Glancing over her shoulder, she saw that Sister Serena was standing by the door with her head modestly lowered.

Close to the warming fire, Arthur was sleeping, curled into a red ball of plush winter fur.

Before she could banish the thought, Eleanor concluded that the cat might be of greater protection for the maid than the young nun. She quickly begged forgiveness of God—but also not too much. Charity was one thing; reality was another.

"While I attend to some other matters, Sister Serena will remain here to keep you company," Eleanor said. "I will send for Brother Thomas, and he will immediately arrange for your safety." She smiled with benevolence to avoid revealing her second intention and said: "Should you need God's comfort, he can provide that as well."

"How can I ever thank you for that kindness?"

By telling me the whole truth, Eleanor said to herself. The offer of the monk was meant as more than a kindness. Jennet might admit a few extra details to a priest than to another woman, even one who was a prioress. The maid seemed more likely to fear for her soul and would be disinclined to lie to a priest, even if an official confession was not begged. A prioress might be formidable, but to some she was still just another woman of rank. Like most servants, as Eleanor well knew, Jennet had probably lied on occasion to Eda and thus would to her as well.

27

Thomas suspected the content of the message to him as soon as he saw the lay sister hurrying down the path, but he also concluded that her speed was more likely due to the cold than great urgency. He hugged his cloak closer to his own shivering body and knew he could not stand still either.

He ran to meet her, his breath chasing his words with a cloud of warm mist. "Our prioress needs my services?"

She did not want to stop so turned around and gestured for him to follow while she explained. "That she does, Brother. She has just finished speaking with the maid of the Countess of Ness. The poor lass is afraid she might be the next victim, and our prioress thinks she might have cause. You are to find her a safer place to stay than the chamber of her dead mistress." Then she looked over her shoulder and grinned. "The maid may also need the solace of a priest, for our lady said the girl might be burdened with secrets she cannot tell anyone else."

Clenching his teeth to stop them from chattering, Thomas grinned back. He knew this lay sister, a woman who had been in service to Tyndal Priory since she became a young widow, and was aware that she held their prioress in high regard. Prioress Eleanor did not need to say much to get the meaning of her messages to him if this lay sister was the bearer.

Jennet fell to her knees when Brother Thomas entered the audience chamber.

Sister Serena fled and positioned herself near the steps just outside the door to the prioress's quarters.

As he gave the expected blessing, he studied the maid. She was shaking.

That could not be due to the cold since there was a good fire in the room and the close-fitting shutters kept the outside air from seeping in. The guilty were often clever enough to feign innocence well, but Thomas did not think that Jennet was sly enough to be that artful. If she shivered, he suspected the cause was her belief that she might die. Finding that one had been close to a murder victim was reason enough to be fearful.

"Come sit at the table, child," he said and directed her to the bench. "Would you like some wine?"

She shook her head vigorously. "Prioress Eleanor said you might find a safe haven for me, Brother. I am so terrified! My mistress has been foully slain. Her priest as well. And some vile imp is following me. I swear it! I have seen his shadow!"

As she went on to list all the places she had smelled the sulfurous reek of evil, Thomas concluded she might not have imagined all of this. Until they knew the reason the two victims had been killed, she could well be in danger. Jennet was the countess's maid, and maids were often the confidant of the mistress. She might not even be aware that she knew an important detail that could solve the crime. But the murderer would not chance allowing her to live long enough to possibly recall it.

He knew of one place to take her that no one with murderous intent might think of or would dare enter if they did. Now he needed to question the maid to get information useful to his prioress, and then he would take the maid to safety.

He raised a hand to stop her increasingly imaginative litany. "I shall find you sanctuary," he said, "but I can only do so if you are innocent of wickedness yourself." He smiled to soften the words enough to comfort and encourage disclosure. "Confession with resultant forgiveness could come later, but I must know first if this murderer has a reason to kill you as well as your mistress and her priest." He bent forward as if staring into her soul through her eyes. "What are you hiding, child? I know there is something, and if I can see that, be assured that God sees far more."

She began to weep.

"Speak," he said with a tone that honestly promised compassion. "Of course God knows everything about you. No place in your heart is deep enough to hide from Him. But you must let Him know that you regret all crimes and long to face penance. He is love, and He is forgiveness."

She reached out to grab his arm, then remembered his vocation and pulled her hand back. "A crime, yes! But I dare not reveal it, or I shall die!"

"Does it involve murder?" He prayed not. Although he could not see how such a timorous woman could kill another human, there was always poison, which was often the choice of the fearful villain. Fortunately, neither of these recent deaths involved that weapon.

"Never! Yet I could still be hanged for what I have done."

"Tell me. If it is not murder, then I may be able to help you, especially if what you tell me reveals a killer."

She shook her head. "It could not. It will only kill me."

"Let me be the judge of that." His voice dropped even lower to a whisper.

Covering her face, she wailed in agony, then stopped and tried to breathe. "I am a thief. I have been stealing jewelry, little things I did not think would be missed too quickly." She shook with wide-eyed fear. "I do not want to hang, Brother!" Then she opened her mouth as if to scream.

"Hush! Calm yourself! But you must answer me if mercy is to be granted. Did you do this to enrich yourself? For how long have you been committing the crime?"

She looked at him in shock, then slowly closed her mouth. "Never for myself, and I would not have been doing it much longer." Her supply of tears apparently consumed, she gazed at Thomas with the longing of the desperate.

He also knew she hoped she didn't have to say any more. "Explain."

Jennet gulped. "It was for my older sister. She was left an impoverished widow just over a year ago. She has young children who would starve without money to feed them. I filched a few small items and sold them to a man in Scotland who would buy with no questions. He paid me little enough but swore to remain silent. It was still enough to keep my sister and babes alive."

Her increased trembling suggested there was far more to this sad tale. He gestured to her to continue. Might he need to know who this buyer was or how she found a source to sell stolen things?

"But she is remarrying soon, Brother. I have stolen my last item."

Did he believe she would steal no more? Now that her mistress was dead, she likely feared for her own survival. Or did she know that the Earl of Ness would provide for her? "And you will swear that on the cross?"

"With no hesitation, Brother, but I beg you not to ask more! My mistress and her priest were not murdered because I stole a few trinkets."

"Yet I must hear the entire tale, Jennet, and even I know you have not revealed all. God will not be satisfied with half-truths."

The next words were whispered so softly that Thomas had to bend closer to hear.

"My mistress caught me. She threatened to expose my crimes and told me that meant the scaffold. I swear I did not kill her, but anyone who knows this will conclude I must have done so to save my neck from the hangman."

"Perhaps she did not mean the threat?" He doubted that but hoped he could learn more by suggesting it. The maid certainly had a motive, but had she really committed the crime? Even more of a question was whether she could have strangled the priest. He looked at her hands and bit back a sigh. They were strong enough to have done it, but he still doubted she was violent. He then silenced the whisper in his soul that reminded him of a fundamental fact. Unless one wanted to die, everyone was capable of murder if their lives were in danger or those of loved ones.

"She meant what she threatened. She was known to ferret out damning secrets about people and tell our local bishop in Scotland. He would then reveal them publicly in his sermons to illustrate the wickedness of mortals. Reputations were destroyed. Some committed self-murder. Most of those exposed were of far higher rank than mine, and clemency was possible, but my birth was too base for mercy."

"How did she catch you and when?"

"I was hiding something I had stolen. She saw me, then

160

demanded I show it to her and tell her from whom I had taken it. This was while we were in court, and I assumed she would wait until our return to Scotland before she revealed my crime to the bishop. But she might have sent him a message. I did not know."

"She only told this particular cleric?"

She nodded.

"What had you stolen?"

Jennet looked away. "It was the necklace with the cross that Prioress Eleanor found near the body of my mistress. You see how terrible this looks. Yet I swear on any remaining hope of God's mercy I might still have that I did not kill her."

"Did you leave it there with her body?"

"No!"

Thomas knew that wail came from too deep within the woman not to be true. "Then why might she have it with her?"

"I do not know. She said she knew the rightful owner and would return it when she was back in Scotland. When I saw Prioress Eleanor pick it up, I knew any claim I would make for innocence was doomed, but I have no idea why she would have taken it with her to that chapel."

"Then tell me from whom you stole it." If the countess did not have it with her and Jennet hadn't dropped it accidentally or deliberately, then someone might well have put it there to suggest a killer. Nor did Thomas dismiss the possibility that the real murderer has dropped it by accident either.

"The Earl of Ness. I was desperate to find one more thing to sell and slipped into his room. It was hidden in his chest. It was a small item, and I thought it odd he would have a woman's necklace. It was not well worn, nor was he in the habit of buying his wife gifts. But it was an easy size for me to hide, and I thought it might bring me just enough.

Since we were at court, I felt safer because he would assume someone there had stolen it if he found it missing."

Perhaps Jennet didn't realize the implications, but Thomas did. Had the earl bought this for someone else? Had his wife understood what it meant? Had she intended to confront her husband with proof of his infidelity in the chapel? Might he have needed to kill her for what she knew? Yet so many couples did have unhappy marriages, and men were usually openly casual about their infidelities. Why would this situation be any different?

"Please, Brother, believe me. I would have run away to avoid the hangman. I never would have killed my mistress."

And although the necklace might cast suspicion on both the earl and the maid, it did not explain who killed the priest or why.

"Did Father Fithian know about this?"

"I doubt it. She might have mentioned it in confession, but it was not her sin. It was mine. And if she had, he might have come to me, as you did, and promise absolution if I confessed. He cared most about souls."

Was it not more likely, Thomas thought, that the priest would have killed the countess if she discovered his own secret? Yet was he any more likely to kill than this maid? The Church must have allowed him to be a priest, and surely he could have found another position if the countess could not bear to keep him on. And if she discovered that he had changed his designated sex for love of the dead crusader, he could still flee to a place he was unknown. Maybe Fithian did not believe he could, but men had committed far greater crimes and found places to live in secret.

The questions continued to circle back on themselves. Who killed the priest? He didn't think Jennet had. If priests were killed over things spoken and held in sacred silence during confession, the world would soon be devoid of priests. Besides, he suspected she hadn't said a word to him if she really had planned to run away.

"Did anyone else know about her way of finding secrets and then telling them to this Scottish bishop? Might that person have had cause to kill her? Think, Jennet!"

"I don't know, Brother! Those whose lives have been destroyed may have cause, but they are in Scotland. The earl and his wife came south with only their servants."

Thomas felt as if his head was going to explode. He must talk to his prioress, but he had one more question. Then he had to move this maid to the promised safe place.

"Another piece of jewelry was found near the body of Father Fithian. I do not have it with me, but it was a man's ring. Not well worn. Simple in design. It had a small ruby in the center and engraving on both sides."

Jennet gasped. "Prioress Eleanor showed it to me. At the time, I was too upset to think properly. Now my memory has returned, and I believe he did have two rings. One he wore almost daily, but the band was worn and the ruby quite large. The ring your prioress showed me had a thistle engraved on one side and a small dragon on the other. The ruby was small. Was it that one you mean?"

Thomas nodded.

"I did not deliberately steal that one. I found it on the floor just outside my master's room. When I picked it up, I decided to keep it in case the necklace did not result in sufficient coin to feed my sister and her family until her marriage. Yes, I thought it might belong to my master, but I forced myself to conclude it did not and the owner would assume it was simply lost. Later, I heard him say he had lost it, but I still said nothing. Then someone stole it from me, Brother. I had hidden it in the straw of my bed. It was there when I rose to accompany my mistress to that terrible chapel." Jennet flushed. "When Prioress Eleanor searched my mistress's quarters after the murder, she found a brooch, but not the ring. At the time, I was too upset to recall that the ring should have been there too. Is that detail helpful?"

He kindly nodded, concluding that it might be. "And afterwards?"

"I did not think more on that until now."

Believing he had enough from the maid, Thomas decided to take her confession to ease her soul. Indeed, she had nothing more to tell him that he could not reveal.

As soon as he had given penance and blessed Jennet, he took her to the anchoress who agree to keep her in the anchorage, safe behind a thick locked door and even thicker stone walls. When Anchoress Juliana took the young woman by the hand, Jennet almost fainted with awe.

That task accomplished, Thomas hurried off to find Prioress Eleanor.

28

The prioress was with her cousin in his quarters.

David might have been the Earl of Ness, thus forgiven much, but he had committed one unpardonable sin to the wrong person. He had not just lied to his cousin, an act deemed base enough within any family, he had done so in her capacity as the head of Tyndal Priory while she was investigating a murder.

"Sit, Cousin, and drink from that cup you hold," she said in a voice that would make angels tremble. "You will need it by the time I am done."

He looked at the goblet, next at his cousin, and then at Brother Thomas standing beside her. Were he to choose the one he feared the most, it would not be the tall, broad-shouldered monk.

He sipped the wine and sat.

"Shall I begin with a list of all the things you have lied about and move on to what I suspect you have simply failed to tell me, or will you do as your mother would have demanded and tell the truth about everything? I have no more patience with petty games and silly pride. Your wife and her priest have been slaughtered in a place dedicated to

God. Your failure to speak like an honest man makes you an accessory to blasphemy."

He bristled, felt his face turn hot, and clutched the goblet until the metal cut into a finger. The worst cause of the pain came because he knew she was right.

Swallowing half of what remained of the wine, David forced himself to look his cousin in the eye. Her gaze seared his flesh more than fire could. If he had ever doubted she was God's right hand, he now repented his error.

"I recognized both the necklace and the ring," he said. "The necklace I bought as a gift for a friend while I was attending King Edward's court. I did so in return for the gift of that ring from the same person."

"Why not say so?"

"Because the friend is a married woman who has been more of a loving wife to me than Eda ever was."

Eleanor said nothing. Her silence was eloquent enough.

David would not have hesitated to say more had he and his cousin been alone, but he worried about the monk hearing what he must now reveal. He had more than one reason to keep his secret well hidden. Of course he understood why the man was here. David knew he was the prime suspect in the murder of his wife as well as that of Father Fithian. But cousins might safely speak of things even when treason was involved. Brother Thomas, however, was no kinsman.

"Brother Thomas and I own a kinship of the spirit," she said. "You speak to him as you must to me."

And now his cousin could read minds? When she died, David thought, God might show His perfect wisdom by appointing her the judge of souls whenever He needed rest. No soul could ever hide even the smallest sin from her.

"I do not know exactly where to start in this chronicle." He lifted his hand. "With the worst, of course. The rest will flow faster if I do." He closed his eyes and finished the remaining wine. As he lowered the goblet, he felt a hand remove it. Brother Thomas had taken it to refill from the ewer close by.

"Your wish to protect her reputation is admirable, Cousin."

"She is not only married, she is wed to a man who is a known enemy of King Edward."

Eleanor swallowed a gasp.

Brother Thomas almost dropped the full goblet of wine but managed to put it down near David instead.

"This was not the case when she and I first fell in love many years ago. Her husband did not care what she did as long as we were discreet. His interests in bed partners lay elsewhere. Then he became involved with a few men who hated the English king. Our own King Alexander III was too busy seeking solace after the death of his queen to notice the whispering, but King Edward learned the Scots might have hopes of assassinating him anyway. Had our English king not known, I would have found a way to warn him, but he has taken the necessary precautions. I found no reason to involve myself."

"And this wife?"

He noted with relief that she did not ask for her name. "Do you not agree that a wife usually suffers from the sins of her husband, even if she is ignorant and innocent of his crimes?"

Eleanor nodded. "So if it were discovered that you were her longtime lover, you would be in grave danger yourself. Were you ever close to her husband?"

"We knew each other. Our families did too, as all families of similar rank do. But he and I had nothing in common and did not spend time together. That relationship was not one that would raise King Edward's doubts about my loyalty.

But you are right. Were it revealed that I was the wife's lover, that might well spark his suspicions." He stopped and drank more wine. "You understand why I did not reveal that I recognized the necklace and from whom the ring came. Yes, I wished to continue our successful attempt to keep our relationship quiet for propriety's sake, although a few surely must suspect. I also saw danger for you and your family if it were to become known that your beloved cousin was, as it were, sleeping with the enemy. My loyalty to King Edward is firm, but after the rebellion of the Welsh, our king might not be in the mood to put great trust in others who had sworn loyalty oaths only to abandon them. His choice of execution for the Welsh prince reveals much about how he thinks these days. It is not the time to offend him if one is wise."

"You must truly love her, David. Most men would have found a safer woman to bed by now."

He knew he was blushing. "She begged me to do as you just said. I could not. To turn from her would be like self-murder. We are of one soul."

"You are like your mother. Once her heart was won, she married your father and no other man tempted her."

"And when he died, she chose to remarry, but only to God."

Eleanor smiled and raised an eyebrow.

"When Eda locked the door to her bedroom, I tried chastity, but I am no monk. I was fortunate to find the woman I did who loves me well." He shook his head. "I am not like my mother," he added. "I tried not to look outside my marriage for solace and failed, but I have not been unfaithful to..." He looked away.

"I am in no doubt about your loyalty to King Edward, and I choose to trust that your lady is of like fealty. I also understand your hesitancy about admitting knowledge of the jewels. Yet how did these two items appear near the two victims? I must also ask, as you will understand, if you killed one or both?"

He shook his head with weariness. "Cousin, even if I were tempted to murder my wife, I would never do so in your priory. And I have no reason at all for killing a priest! I am innocent of both murders and as confused as you are over why these items were found at the scene of the deaths."

"Have you more to tell me?"

"There is one thing, but it does not answer that question about the jewels."

"Perhaps that you had managed to hide your long relationship with another woman from your wife until recently?"

He blinked. "If she did know, I assumed she did not care —or rather that it was of no value to her. Recently, however, she announced to me that she did know. When she told me this, she said she cared only that I had sinned so grievously against God and King Edward. She threatened to reveal the relationship. Doing so would bring the wrath of the king down on my head as well as all the other grief I have mentioned before." He drank some more wine. "I begged her to rethink this revelation and obviously omitted the probable suffering of my beloved or me, but I emphasized the impact on our children."

"What did she say?"

"Nothing. Yet for all her coldness to most mortals, she loved our children. I do not read souls well, but I did have a little hope that she might have mercy on them and remain silent."

"Do you know if she told anyone about this secret before her death?"

"I believe she was waiting to return home to do so. Her favored cleric for revelations was our local bishop and she gained much joy from telling him directly about her discoveries."

"You realize that this makes you a greater suspect in killing your wife."

David rested his elbows on his knees and opened his hands in a plea for mercy. "If I were guilty, why would I leave items that pointed to me as a murderer? I am not that stupid. And how did the person get the items in the first place? The ring I thought I might have lost, but I had the necklace hidden in my travel chest to give to my lady when I returned to Scotland."

"And Father Fithian's death?"

"I had nothing against the man except his stench. And most found it vile including those of us who spent months living with other crusaders in the Holy Land, men who steamed with sweat until their armor rusted and also lacked the water to cleanse let alone drink. But I would not kill a man just because he was as rank as a privy."

Eleanor knew where the necklace and ring had originally been found by Jennet, why she had taken them, but not why the items were found near the corpses. The most significant question remained. Who had stolen them from Jennet and planted them by the corpses? Had the killer wanted to point the finger of guilt at Jennet or David? Or did it even matter as long as the killer escaped detection? Was this ploy meant to gain time for escape? And why kill the two victims here and not someplace else, including the road back to Scotland?

"Do you have any further questions of me?"

Her cousin may have lied and also held back things he ought to have revealed, but she understood why. He was an honorable man, often to his own detriment. This was what she would have expected from him, and thus she felt he was finally telling the truth. Others might not conclude David was innocent from this, but Eleanor felt confident that he was. Her heart softened, and her mind was satisfied with the logic of it all.

"Nothing more for now, Cousin. As for what you have told me in confidence about your longtime love, I hope that it may stay a secret. Should it be revealed, I will lend my voice to your support, as well as that of your lady. Yet keep in mind that my woman's voice may be worth little in the king's court." What she did not add was her intention to enlist the help of her elder brother, Baron Hugh, if required.

"For your confidence and understanding, I am deeply grateful. If I recall anything more, whether or not I believe it significant, I shall come to you." He smiled but was too weary to sustain it for long. "If I were guilty of murder, I would confess it and pray that you would grant me the mercy of your blessing before I was hanged." Once again, he bowed his head. "There is a question you have not asked which I will answer. My wife's body must be taken to Scotland for burial. Whatever sins we both committed, and especially those against each other, she was still the Countess of Ness and Scotland's daughter."

"Then our priory will prepare her body for the journey, Cousin. As for your guilt, I have no doubt about your innocence and if required, I will stand as a witness to your character and innocence."

He stood and bowed. "I am grateful for your confidence! Now I may find a well-populated chapel in which to pray before I take some rest. I have no wish for solitude but will sleep with an armed guard and my sword nearby. I survived surprise attacks while on crusade. I am not an easy man to kill should this villain try to murder me too."

"The hospital chapels are rarely empty," she said, "although the church for the village has frequent visitors if you prefer that despite the weather. Should you wish, I could send a lay brother to accompany you."

"I thank you, dear Cousin, but I do not want to trouble a lay brother who must have many more important tasks assigned by the prior".

As he turned to leave for prayer, his expression became puzzled, and he stopped. "An irrelevant question, but one that raises my curiosity. Where did Prior Vincent come from? Has he been here long? He reminds me of a man I met years ago. I did not know him well and cannot recall the name..." He waved his hand dismissively. "It is not important. Just idle curiosity."

In fact, Eleanor did not know the answers to his questions. The prior had been here when she arrived herself as a young woman of twenty. And until he was elected prior after Prior Andrew's death, she had had no cause to notice or care about the man. Unless there was good reason to do otherwise, she had always let the prior rule the few monks the priory had.

"I will ask," she replied with a smile as she and Brother Thomas followed him. She was also grateful David had reminded her that the prior might be a witness who could confirm her cousin was not near the chapel when the priest was slain. Prior Vincent's testimony would be vital to establish innocence.

29

Back in her audience chamber with Ralf, Sister Anne, and Brother Thomas, Eleanor gave the crowner an abbreviated report on the conversations with Jennet and the Earl of Ness. Before Ralf arrived, the monastic trio had agreed that a few of the secrets revealed by the maid and David might be left unspoken, at least for the time being.

Sister Anne had been more hesitant. Those secrets gave both Jennet and David cause to kill Eda in view of the woman's ardent fondness for discovering and revealing details that resulted in severe suffering for many.

Eleanor concurred but had sworn to let the crowner know if more facts suggested the king's man must hear more details. She was not happy to have to keep information from her friend either. They had always been honest with each other, but she suspected that Ralf might be happier not knowing that Jennet was a thief considering the reasons she had committed the crimes. For all his gruffness, the crowner had a soft heart. As for David's tenuous link to enemies of the English king, she feared Ralf might not be so sympathetic. So why put him into a quandary about his duty to the king when she was convinced her cousin was completely innocent of any crime against Edward?

Keeping the crowner ignorant of the thefts and an unlikely link to treason seemed the wiser path for all involved.

Ralf scowled. "I understand that your cousin is an honorable man who wants to protect the virtue of his mistress. But surely he could have told you early on about the necklace and later the ring instead of denying he recognized them. He may be guilty of adultery, but was it worth becoming a suspect in a crime that would lead him to the hangman? He does not know me, but you could have assured him that I would keep his secret if needed. His sin is common enough for men."

Eleanor had never made the mistake of taking the crowner for a fool. "Remember, Ralf, that he is much older than I and still thinks of me as that little girl who clung to his mother's arm when he visited Amesbury. I was quite aware of his thinking but believed I could persuade him in a private conversation that I was now fully grown and might hear tales not usually told a child." She laughed. "And I was right."

"You think he is innocent, then? You are not troubled by the presumed coincidence that both items belonging to him were found by the murder sites?"

"He claims they were both stolen from him."

"As was his knife," Thomas added.

"Very convenient." Ralf tipped his head and gazed at both monk and prioress with no attempt to hide his disbelief.

"When I went with him to search his room after his wife's murder," Thomas said, "he seemed angry that the knife was missing, then grieved and perplexed by what he called a theft. A guilty man might point an accusing finger at

174

someone. He might be flustered as he came up with lies. But outrage? Grief?"

"Maybe he had an accomplice and was in rage because the hired assassin was stupid enough to leave such an obvious clue behind?"

"Oh, Ralf, you are making this entire thing too complicated. We are beginning to move from a single killer of a woman and a priest toward a plot that might have enough murderers to be the envy of kings in a power struggle." Eleanor waved her hand to dismiss the entire idea. "Do you really think that there are accomplices?"

"Despite our disagreement about which of us has the authority here," Ralf replied, "I have always been inclined to think your cousin was innocent. Not because he is of high rank and, according to my elder brother, well respected at court for his military skills, but because I hold your understanding of mortals in high regard." His expression suggested he was holding back a smile. "Even cousins."

Eleanor nodded appreciation for his compliment. Of course he had consulted with his brother, she thought, and was glad he had done so.

"I do not think your cousin is a man lacking wits. How many murderers not only leave the murder weapon, so obviously owned by themselves, in the victim's chest, but happily scatter other evidence leading back to them at both sites? Not one site, which might be deemed a true accident, but both? This makes me think that the killer wanted to implicate your cousin so much he almost bludgeoned us with hints."

"We are in agreement, Ralf," she said.

He raised his hand. "Yet! The items did belong to him, and he can only claim they were stolen. A clever man might well do such an obviously stupid thing to make us think he must be innocent in the way I explained."

"Jennet says that she heard him complain to someone that this particular ring was missing. He believed he might have dropped it. This occurred at court," Thomas added.

"And why did she fail to tell us that she recognized both objects as belonging to your cousin?" Ralf eyes were narrowed with skepticism.

"Because she is a loyal servant who would never let vile suspicion fall on a much-appreciated master." Eleanor hoped that would satisfy her friend.

"And her explanations of why we should not suspect her of one or two murders?"

"What reason had she? Her mistress demanded no more than any other. The priest was fair in his penances. She was with Father Fithian when her mistress was killed. They had been told to wait outside the chapel. I questioned them at the time. And, once again, if she or my cousin were clearly innocent of one crime, why think either was guilty of the other?"

"So where are we now in solving these murders?" There was no sarcasm in the crowner's tone, but he did sound weary.

"Although the conclusion that my cousin is innocent may still be on very shaky ground, I feel I have made some progress in taking a little of the burden of guilt from him." She waited for a reaction. "There may also be a witness to prove he could not have killed the priest."

"And this witness is...?"

"I would prefer to keep the name to myself for the moment, Ralf. I must be the one to question him since he is under my authority. Should he prove useful, you may talk with him."

After a long hesitation, the crowner nodded.

"As for Jennet, she has no alibi or witness to prove she is

innocent of the priest's murder, but she and Father Fithian were together when my cousin's wife was killed."

"And she might have killed the priest if he decided to change his story in support of that tale or recalled she had vanished for a little while. A call of nature?"

"This killing might have been committed by a woman." Sister Anne broke her silence, and her face was deathly pale.

"Well noted," Eleanor replied softly. She knew the nun's silence about the maid's theft and the treasonous nature of the spouse of the earl's mistress had been difficult, but they had all agreed that other aspects must be mentioned.

"Any benefit to either if the countess and the priest are dead?" Ralf looked longingly at the ewer on a nearby table.

Suddenly, Sister Serena burst from her utterly motionless position by the door, grabbed the jug, and filled a cup of wine for the crowner. He was so grateful, he ignored how much slopped onto his knee when she shoved it into his hand.

The prioress winced but flashed an approving smile at the young nun as she hurried back to assume her pose of a silent but awkward statue. "None for either if the priest is dead." She prayed her phrasing was subtle enough to pass the crowner's notice. "He was known to keep the secrets of the confessional in his heart. And the death of her mistress means Jennet has no position at the moment, although my cousin will likely find her something to feed and house her. As for my cousin, it makes no difference if Eda is dead. My cousin still cannot marry his mistress because her husband is alive."

Ralf sighed. "We have nothing, then."

"There is still the unanswered question of why the murder of my cousin's wife happened here, not at court, not on the journey from Scotland or the one to our priory, and not even before anyone left Scotland. Another unanswered question is why both the countess and the priest were murdered. What was the connection?" Eleanor looked at each face around her, but none had any more ideas than she did.

"And thus you still wish to retain in command of the investigation?" Ralf finished his wine.

Eleanor appreciated that the question was clearly one of clarification and had no hint of irritation or bitterness. "Ralf, I shall happily turn this entire matter over to you very soon. It was never my intention to keep control out of pride or a desire to protect my cousin whether he was guilty or not. I believed I could more effectively get the truth from him and feel I have done enough in that regard. I do still wonder if there is a reason why Tyndal was chosen for the shedding of blood and if that requires my greater involvement. Therefore, I must speak with the witness who might prove my cousin innocent of Father Fithian's death."

"Then I may summon my men to enter the priory and question the secular people who were here at the time of the murders?"

"Please wait just a little longer, Ralf. Talking to the witness will not take me long." She hesitated and looked down at the rushes. "I have one more thing to do before I do that. Something I have put aside far too long."

"May I ask what that is?"

"A small thing," she said, then looked around with a determined expression. "I must make peace with a longtime foe."

30

When Eleanor entered the small private quarters usually assigned to a sub-prioress, she did so quietly.

Sister Ruth lay propped up in her bed, eyes shut. Sister Christina, the priory infirmarian, sat by her side, bowed her head in prayer, and held the aged patient's hand.

Eleanor's first thought was that her nemesis and former sub-prioress had died despite Sister Anne's encouraging news. Pressing a hand against her heart, she felt tears, burning with salt, collect in her eyes. She had come too late! She would never forgive herself for setting aside this visit for reasons that seemed so petty in retrospect, and she was angry for coming now mostly because she needed information. Could there ever be enough time in any day to seek forgiveness or make amends for such selfishness?

But Sister Christina saw her and smiled, that ethereal expression which added to her reputation as a saint in the making. Gently, she released her patient's hand and gestured for her prioress to join her just outside the door.

"How is she?" Eleanor asked once they had left the chamber. Apart from guilt over her failure to come earlier,

Eleanor's concern was genuine. She had many reasons not to like Sister Ruth, but she never denied the woman's many organizational skills. And she had long sympathized with a woman, legitimately elected leader of this priory, who had been forced from the position because a twenty-year-old with no experience whose family had found favor with King Henry III was chosen to take her place by royal decree.

Not long after she had arrived, and learned the full effects of King Henry III's decision, Eleanor picked Sister Ruth to be her sub-prioress, a decision that shocked many, probably including the nun. Nonetheless, the two women had worked together uneasily yet well until Sister Ruth resigned for reasons that said much about the older woman's deep sense of honor. Since then, Eleanor had not found anyone else in her flock who was as competent to take on that position, a failure for which she was paying an increasingly high price.

Eleanor needed to say much to this nun before she died. She could not lie and say she loved her as a fellow religious. But she must acknowledge the woman's devotion to God's service despite legitimate anger and disappointment. Eleanor suspected that Sister Ruth had never stopped hating her, and they viewed the world in completely different ways, but Eleanor wondered if she could have devoted herself to serving Sister Ruth with the same competence and dedication if the circumstances had been reversed.

Eleanor also knew she must express her gratitude and get the information she needed in a short time. She had no wish to send Sister Ruth more swiftly to God by exhausting her.

"God has been gracious, my lady," Sister Christina said. "Death hovered close to our beloved sister for some time, but God must have sent him away to claim other souls. Sister Ruth seems to be recovering."

Squeezing her eyes shut for a brief prayer of thankfulness, Eleanor felt a surge of relief. "Your prayers in particular have been of great help, Sister."

"She has benefited from the pleas of the entire priory, my lady." The infirmarian lowered her head modestly. "It was you who asked everyone to pray for her. It was you who ordered that she be brought to these quarters, away from curious eyes and for her greater comfort."

As any prioress should do, Eleanor thought and bit her lip. There had been no special merit in performing her duty. "Few recover from apoplexy," she added.

"Sister Anne now believes it was a minor attack. She cannot say how long the illness will continue to plague her, how paralyzed she may remain, or if she will suffer another episode."

"May I speak to her without greatly adding to her weariness? I fear I have some private questions only she can answer."

Sister Christina frowned but then brightened. "It is possible, my lady. I see just behind you that a lay sister has arrived at the door with some sustenance from the kitchen. I must wake Sister Ruth. Our sub-infirmarian has ordered her to eat at least some sustaining nourishment." She lowered her voice. "I do not tell our revered elder sister that Sister Anne requires it. Instead, I say that God demands she do so." Her eyes twinkled. "Surely He does and thus saves me from committing a wicked falsehood."

Eleanor returned the woman's smile. Apart from this nun's evident piety and the many paeans to her virtues as a healer with her prayers, the prioress respected the infirmarian for her humility and support for her more secular-oriented assistant, Sister Anne. When others cast doubt on the practices of the former apothecary, Sister Christina replied: "Satan destroys. He does not heal. So if Sister Anne's methods reduce death and suffering, I must conclude that only God guides her hand and enlightens her wits."

As the infirmarian gestured for the lay sister with the meal with a tempting smell to enter, Eleanor remained outside and waited for Sister Christina to return.

It did not take long. The infirmarian bent around the door and asked Eleanor to enter. "Do not spend too much time," she said. "She seemed eager to see you when I said you had a few questions and even promised to eat more if she was allowed to talk with you."

"I will do my best not to weary her, but please warn me if I fail to notice the signs," Eleanor replied and entered the room with a smile for the patient.

Sister Ruth had always been short of stature but broad in hip and thick of waist. Her only thinness was in her lips. They were habitually formed into a moue of disapproval, a harsh judgment of the world that was reinforced by her squinting small eyes filled with intense disdain for whatever she was gazing upon. As Eleanor eventually learned, the fierce squint was the result of extremely poor distance vision but probably still expressed the nun's general view of mortals.

But the woman lying in the bed was diminished in both form and zeal. Eleanor found herself deeply missing the ardent and energetic curmudgeon.

"My lady! How kind of you to visit me!" Sister Ruth tried an uncharacteristic smile but could only form the expression with half her mouth. "Sister Christina told me you have asked for daily reports and even prayed by my side."

The reports Eleanor had asked for, but she had come by only once after Sister Ruth had been stricken. As for this room, it had been on Sister Anne's advice that she had ordered the nun moved from the general hospital to these empty quarters she had once occupied and where she could escape the moans of the dying and the wails of their kin.

"And," the nun's voice dropped to a harsh whisper, "I learned that you have allowed Sister Christina to stay by my side so I might benefit from her healing prayers." Her one eye turned heavenward. Her other eye struggled to halfway match its twin.

Of course I did, Eleanor thought. After discussing the patient's care with both the infirmarian and her assistant, they all agreed that Sister Anne's "potions and lotions", as Sister Ruth contemptuously named them, might work, but they would be far more effective if given with Sister Christina's hand and accompanied by her prayers.

"I will not stay long now for I do not wish to tire you," Eleanor said.

"You have questions for me?"

Eleanor noticed with surprise that the nun's eyes shone with unusual pleasure. The prioress was also encouraged to note that her speech had remained fairly clear. That bodes well for a better recovery, she thought. She was also grateful because that meant she was not in danger of prolonging the visit by frequent requests for clarification of Sister Ruth's answers.

"Our priory has suffered from violence once again. We seek a quick resolution so we may purge our sacred ground of the pollution and return uninterrupted to our duty of serving God. Only you can provide me with details that might well lead us to this desired resolution." Eleanor reached out and rested her hand briefly on Sister Ruth's bone-thin arm.

Sister Ruth looked at her with a fleeting expression of gratitude. Eleanor knew she had not imagined it. As she had become aware, mortals often briefly shed the pettiness of everyday life when Death chose to turn his back on them. The moment would not last, but in this one tiny instant, the two of them could feel a kinship of purpose untainted by their feuds and resentments.

"I need you to tell me what you know about Brother Vincent's life before he took vows with our Order of Fontevraud." She deliberately omitted his current title. The older woman might not have heard of his very recent election, and giving her an explanation would take time and only tire her unduly.

"Is he a suspect?" The nun's effort to scowl failed.

"I have no reason to think so, but something may have occurred in his early life that could be significant. When he begged admission here, he must have given some account of his life and why he discovered his vocation. He might not recognize the importance of details to our current purpose or have even forgotten too many over time. You, however, would not."

Sister Christina gestured to Eleanor to let her encourage the patient to eat a little more. After Sister Ruth had dutifully done so, the infirmarian moved the pillows into a more comfortable and supportive position.

"Enough, sweet child! You spoil me. But do remove this food. Sister Matilda has long fed us far too well, but she sent a sinful amount to me, all of which ought to have been given to the poor of the village." She shooed the uneaten portion away with her good hand.

The infirmarian looked at the amount eaten, then nodded to the prioress with a quick smile.

With relief, Eleanor interpreted this to mean that Sister Ruth had edged closer to committing that feared sin of gluttony than she had ever done before.

The food whisked away to presumably feed the poor, the

elder nun folded her hands over the blanket and said, "You did not ask, but I will start by telling you that Brother Vincent, from his entry to this priory, has been a truly pious man. Therefore I am being unkind, and shall confess my wickedness shortly, when I say he has also been a very dull one. When he first arrived, Prioress Felicia and I both thought he had a hint of the Devil's own splendor about him. Many a lay sister and not a few nuns gazed just long enough on him to sin in their hearts. But he ignored them and has always exhibited exemplary virtue. Few monks have prayed so much or for so long. His sincerity was proven when he chose his solitary devotions during times most would not see him performing them. When he fainted from lack of sleep, Prior Theobald was forced to order him to cut back on his devotions. Brother Vincent obeyed but only minimally. His habits and piety have never changed in all the years I have been aware of him."

"And before he came here?"

"I did not know him, but my brother, may God have mercy on his soul, did. Not well because of their disparity in rank, but he relayed some strange stories when he learned of Vincent's arrival. Although it was never proven, some alleged that Vincent had had an affair with a woman of rank while her husband was crusading in the Holy Land. This woman also had a brother who knew her husband and joined him on crusade. My own brother was well acquainted with those two men, but he never mentioned their names because of the scandal. Not long after the woman's brother returned to England he was foully murdered, but the crime was never solved. There was some rumor that Vincent might have been involved in it because he inexplicably vanished soon after. But my brother lost interest in the tales and forgot the man until he heard that Vincent had died."

Died? But Eleanor noticed that the nun was turning pale. She glanced at Sister Christina standing behind the patient. The infirmarian nodded to relay the message that Sister Ruth was becoming fatigued.

"You two needn't conspire." Sister Ruth coughed. "Very little left to say, my lady, and then you may go back to solving this crime as God demands." She took a deep breath. "Vincent did not try to hide the tale of murder and his purported part in it. Prioress Felicia told me that he begged an audience with her and Prior Theobald and told them about it, beginning with the explanation that he had vanished to seek treatment for a mortal illness and that might have led to the belief he had died. When he survived, he knew he had a strong vocation to serve God out of gratitude. As for the crime, he claimed complete innocence. Apparently, he had a cousin to whom he bore a strong resemblance. Although he could not swear to it, he feared this cousin might have done the killing. There was no possibility to question the man because he had since committed self-murder, and his soul was in Hell. Regarding any affair with a married woman, he confessed he committed so many sins out of lust that he could not even remember all the women. His story seemed reasonable. Most certainly, his vocation has proven sincere. His embrace of virtue is unquestioned. That adds credence to his version."

Eleanor waited.

Sister Ruth nodded to indicate she was done.

"You have given me what I need, Sister, as you always have since I arrived. Had it not been for your competence and wisdom, I could not have succeeded in a position for which I had no skill or experience. There has not been a day when I have not thanked God for your help. In this new matter, you have again proved how well you serve God."

Sister Ruth's pallor faded as her cheeks bloomed with an

almost youthful pink. In healthier days, she would not have allowed such a betrayal of pleasure and would have banished the weakness with a gruff demeanor. Her failure was a sad reminder of how sick she was.

Sister Christine walked to the nearby table and poured a potion into a maser of very watered wine. "This first," she said to the nun, "and then we shall pray until God grants you some sleep." She helped the nun drink it down.

Eleanor rose to leave but was stopped by a soft voice from the bed.

"You are deeply in need of sleep yourself, my lady. Even I can see the fatigue. You need a sub-prioress. I may be able to assist you in finding one…"

Eleanor turned around to thank Sister Ruth, but the nun had already fallen asleep.

Sister Christine set the mazer back down on the table and escorted the prioress to the door.

"Stay at her side and pray until she has recovered as much as she can," Eleanor whispered.

"She will thrive most, my lady, because of your visit today. God is well aware of your kindness to our beloved sister."

Eleanor felt as if she had just been blessed by a saint and, feeling deeply unworthy, bowed her head.

When she looked up, Sister Christine had already gone back to her patient.

31

As she carefully walked along the icy path back to her quarters, Eleanor felt an inexplicable lightness she had not experienced in many months.

She was glad that Sister Ruth appeared to be on the mend, although she was fully aware that the improvement might not last. Sister Anne said that apoplexy was a strange disease that often hovered close by and attacked again, usually with greater force and in a more deadly fashion.

Nor did she quite know what the older nun meant when she had said she could help in finding a new sub-prioress. But she had told Sister Ruth how much she had appreciated her, and that she needed to do before the woman died— whenever that might be. Her speech was sincere, although it had required tremendous will to utter it. And it may have taken Sister Ruth a great deal to accept the words she heard from a woman she disliked. Neither of them would ever likely forgive or love the other in what they had been taught was the spirit of their faith, but Eleanor wondered if forgiveness might not have as many definitions as love.

Even if Sister Ruth lived to match the longevity of Methuselah, Eleanor knew they could never see the world the same way and would continue to irritate each other with every breath. Nonetheless, she felt that something might have eased between them today. She prayed it would last, and perhaps the meaning of the difference would grow clearer to her in time.

For the moment, however, she must turn from heavenly compassion to ponder earthly violence.

Eleanor was still uncertain how her cousin might have met Prior Vincent or have had a memorable enough contact, brief though it must have been, that he recognized the changed man so many years later. If David knew either of the two crusaders in the story, that might have been why he had seen him. Yet Vincent did not seem to have recognized David. Or if he had, perhaps he chose not to approach him. The difference in rank might explain the latter, or else he had simply forgotten the earl after a span of many years.

She feared that was the easiest twist in the vague and rumored story. Had Eda been one of the man's conquests? She forced herself to rid her mind of disbelief that Eda could ever have tempted a man so much. The woman had been young once, after all, and likely attractive enough before many babies thickened her waist and caused her breasts to flatten and drop. She shook her head to rid it of such petty thoughts and went back to what she had learned.

If Vincent had slept with so many married women that he could not name them, let alone their husbands, then he might not have recognized David. That was something she could not ignore. She might pray that difference in rank was the cause of the prior's failure to greet her cousin, but she preferred to save her prayers for more realistic hopes.

Eleanor was troubled by much in this tale of lechery. The priest Eleanor knew was quite different from the man who claimed to have lain with any willing woman he found, at least according to Sister Ruth. Without question, there had never been a single rumor about his chastity during the decade she had been prioress here. His appearance must have changed since those days he claimed to have been a strutting rooster with a flock of hens. His body was thin, suggesting a once athletic build, but now he lacked firm muscles and both his neck and chin sagged. Had he lied about his exploits to make his vocation seem stronger? Might he have stolen the alleged cousin's tale and made it his own? And if he had lied, what difference did it make in what she needed to ask him?

Eleanor had at least been right to confirm if there was any connection between the murders and her priory. She believed what Sister Ruth had told her about the prior, but the details still demanded further investigation. As much as Eleanor might abhor this possibility, she feared she must take the possibility seriously that the long-ago mistress with the crusader husband and murdered brother could be Eda. Yet was it really credible that the dead woman, one so obsessed with the sins of others, had had an affair with the now Prior Vincent while David was in the Holy Land?

Yes, it was, she reminded herself. Many frolicking youthful sinners became vituperative religious zealots in later life.

However, David had said nothing about any affair Eda might have had. He might not even know, and his relationship with his wife had been so troubled that it was even possible he did not care. Most men would be horrified to have horns put on their heads, but her cousin might not be one as long as it wasn't flaunted. He had his own lady and kept that relationship secret.

There was also now more she did not know. Sister Ruth had provided a possible link between this priory and Eda's murder, although the connection to the priest's murder remained unclear. All details must be followed and questions answered. She had promised Ralf that she would soon turn over the investigation to him. But she still had reason not to do so as quickly as she had hoped.

It was clear that she must talk with Prior Vincent immediately.

She felt the need to ask for more details about this mysterious cousin who had allegedly died or committed self-murder. Had he done either? Was it possible that he lived and had become an even more invisible lay brother at this priory? Was that the reason Prior Vincent made the unusual choice of coming to this daughter house in the Order of Fontevraud where Eve's daughters ruled Adam's sons? Or had the relative found a home nearby in the secular world? To her knowledge, Prior Vincent did not have visitors, but her knowledge of him was limited. He and any cousin might have met during prayer in the more public church.

She must also find out if the new prior had ever met David and under what circumstances. This would require especially diplomatic questioning. If the prior had left the world with a profound regret over his lust, he might well resist going back to a time he longed to repent and forget. And if he had committed adultery with her cousin's wife and was now forced to reveal it? How could Prior Vincent ever face the Earl of Ness on his visits here? Indeed, this might make her own relationship with the new prior even more fraught. Added to that, should she learn that he had lied to enhance the sincerity of his vocation, they might find it impossible to work together at all.

Whatever the cost, she had to summon him to her chambers without delay. Was she worried about how he might react to her knowledge of his past? Of course she was. For years, he had been pious and even dull, as Sister Ruth had said. Nonetheless, the past might be relevant. She was obliged to pry as well as discover if the man had lied so many years ago. The man's pride was an issue. Pride was one of the seven deadly sins, but she knew how much it wounded to have her own pride hurt. Her aunt had taught her that God demanded it be tossed aside, yet she found it excruciatingly hard to do so. How much harder would be for Prior Vincent, who was prickly by nature at best?

Climbing the stairs to her chambers, she knew she should have Brother Thomas join her, but he must surely be with Master Durant now. She would send a lay sister to summon him but also make it clear that there was no need for hurry and he ought to finish whatever he was doing for the former vintner. It did not matter if he heard the entire story from Prior Vincent. Eleanor could tell him details later, and that might be for the best.

She was fully aware how ill-advised it was to have Brother Thomas there at all, learning troubling secrets about his priory superior. Not that her monk would ever abuse the confidence, and he had always remained subservient to his priors in the past, but Prior Vincent would likely resent him for knowing them and find small ways to punish the monk because he was the prioress's special confidant. That relationship had never been a problem with Prior Andrew, but he was dead.

She might have chosen Sister Anne, but the prior could reasonably refuse to talk in the presence of yet another nun about his adulterous past. A prioress was bad enough, but Eleanor ruled Tyndal. She had the right to ask questions. So Brother Thomas must come, but Eleanor knew she had yet another situation that needed tactful and sensitive handling.

It was best, she decided, if the arrival of Brother Thomas was timed for after any embarrassing revelations were made and discussed. She required his fine counsel, but his special relationship with her did not need what amounted to blaring trumpets while uncomfortable secrets were being pried from Vincent. All the religious here were aware that the monk accompanied her whenever she needed him for local or afar investigations. Much could be ignored as Thomas slipped quickly back into his role of humble priory monk. But Prior Vincent, being humiliated in front of one of his charges, was unlikely to set any of this aside.

A lay sister bowed as Eleanor approached the door to her chambers. She told the woman to seek the prior and tell him that he must attend her immediately. After, the lay sister must find Brother Thomas and give him the message that he should come to her chambers when he was finished with his other required duties.

In the meantime, Eleanor thought, Sister Serena at least had returned to her responsibilities and would provide proper attendance during this meeting. For once, Eleanor didn't have to worry about finding another nun to take her place.

32

Prior Vincent made no attempt to hide his annoyance at the summons. His scowl bordered on the offensive. "I have work to do, my lady. The accounts you gave me to review were not done properly by the last prior and take much time to resolve and correct."

Had she not already reviewed them herself, she might have feared that Prior Andrew had been too feeble before his death to do his usually meticulous work. But even as he approached his deathbed, he had shown care and precision, then confessed it when he no longer could. With the pressures of all her responsibilities rapidly eroding her self-control, she almost told this whining incompetent that he might have understood the rolls better if he knew anything about priory administration.

Instead, she forced herself to turn her back on him and step to the window that looked out over the monastic grounds. As always, the view calmed, but the hot fire crackling behind her was a reminder that God did not tolerate wrath and Satan punished it harshly in the afterlife. She willed herself to summon at least a hint of forgiveness toward this obnoxious man, but her efforts succeeded in only a knife-thin victory.

"This should not take long, Prior Vincent. I have called you here because I think you have some crucial knowledge from your past that might help solve the murders of my cousin's wife and her priest."

He cleared his throat. "I cannot imagine what help I could be, my lady. Surely you were misinformed, or else some imp infected one of your dreams."

She clenched her jaw. No one in her position would allow a subordinate to speak this way without punishment. She might be weary and prone to snappishness, but Prior Vincent had now moved from arrogant peevishness to blatant insolence. She needed the information he had, so she would be firm and demand it first instead of immediately sending him into confinement. But several days publicly separated from his monks while he confessed his errors and received his penance would be forthcoming. How he responded to her orders would determine whether she allowed him to even continue as a prior. It was her right to remove him, although she had long ago decided to use it only in extreme circumstances.

"As your leader here, I need not justify my queries to you, and your tone is offensive, but I shall reply because we are commanded to counter arrogance with kindness, Prior. The Earl of Ness told me that he believed he recognized you and was curious about your past. I knew nothing because you had been here long before I arrived. Earlier today, I asked one of our longest-serving nuns if she knew your background and she told me your tale..."

From behind her, she heard a crash and a woman's cry of pain.

She turned around and saw Sister Serena lying crumpled on the floor.

Prior Vincent was bolting the audience chamber door.

"Do not move, my lady." He looked at her with an expression she had never seen on the face of a sane man. His lips were twisted into an unnatural grin, and his eyes glistened like those of a maniacal hobgoblin.

Taking two steps toward her and blocking any way to the secured door, he drew a knife from his sleeve. "I had hoped, indeed prayed, that this moment would never arrive. I grieve that it has."

This was not the time to analyze how she could have missed sensing danger in this man. She needed all her wits to deal with what had exploded into the likelihood that her soul and that of her young nun would soon be on their way to face God.

"I do not understand," she said, deciding that sounding clueless was wise—not that she found it difficult to portray the truth.

"I had assumed you could be easily led astray in the deaths of Eda and her priest. Her husband was the obvious suspect with their unhappy marriage, and I left enough hints of his guilt that even a woman could see that he had done it." Like some child, he wiggled around in an odd strutting dance. "But I made them just clever enough so you would delude yourself into believing you had been quick-witted, a sin of which you have long been guilty."

"Why?" A broad question, but she was trying to come up with ones requiring more detailed answers to give herself the chance to think. Anything to distract the man and earn time. He was certainly arrogant enough that he might enjoy long explanations. She also wondered if there was any chance she could knock him down. If so, and he dropped his knife, she might have time to unbolt the door and flee. But she could not leave the unconscious nun for him to butcher, and she also feared she was too small to unbalance this man despite his lack of bulk.

He came a little closer, licking his lips as he looked at her.

She felt like a savory piece of venison might just before it was sliced into bites.

"Have you summoned anyone?"

If she denied it, she had some chance of delaying long enough for Brother Thomas to arrive. The door was bolted, but if she shouted for help when he knocked, those broad shoulders of his might be enough to crack the door open. Could all this commotion be enough to distract this mad man just long enough to save Sister Serena and her?

"I had no need," she said in a deliberately trembling voice. "I had Sister Serena for propriety."

"Ooo!" He said in a high-pitched voice. "Sister Serena!" Gesturing with the knife at the prone body on the floor, he actually sang in triumph, "And wasn't she useful as protection?"

Her mind flailing for questions, Eleanor asked, "Why kill my cousin's wife? Didn't everything involving her happen many years ago before you took vows?" She hoped she sounded as if she knew more than she did but was still ignorant. The latter would appeal to his feeling of superiority over her.

"Because she came here and might recognize me, you stupid woman! And she thought I was dead. She might have shouted out the news to any ear, and that would have destroyed all I have spent so much effort and time building in this priory."

Eleanor put a hand over her mouth and opened her eyes as wide as possible. Now the entire story was coming together, and she had no doubt that she was facing a man who had murdered at least twice and would have no qualms

197

about repeating the crime. "So you made my cousin a cuckold!"

"She was a fine woman to bed in those days. Not the lumpy, sad-faced crone I saw in the chapel. And had she not told her brother that she preferred me to her husband in bed, I might simply have gone on to another when your cousin came home. But her brother swore to reveal my name to her husband, a man known to be quick with a sword. I had to kill the fool. It was easy enough to disappear after and not be in fear that your cousin would kill me for putting horns on his head. I arranged for the rumor to be spread that I had died. Then I joined this unnatural Order that no one would think a man known for swyving women would enter." He snorted.

"So you had no vocation?" Eleanor tried to calculate how long it would take her monk to get here, then realized she had lost all sense of time as she fought for her life and that of Sister Serena.

He turned surprisingly pensive. The maniacal expression dimmed for a brief moment. "Not then, yet I did find God here—or He found me. He and I have had many conversations over the years." He smirked as the uneven glitter of madness returned. "You should be terrified to learn how wicked He thinks you are! It was He who guided me on the path to becoming prior and eventually ruling Tyndal. When I did, I planned to have you scrubbing floors in a torn shift and beaten often for your unwomanly arrogance. I shall not now waste time lecturing you on the grave sins you have been committing by perverting the natural order and ruling over men. God will soon send you to Hell for that, although I regret losing the pleasure of seeing you cleaning the garderobes."

"The rules of the Order..."

"Are sinful! God has told me that I am destined to

vanquish the Devil first in this place and later in Anjou!" His voice raised and he flourished his knife, then he stepped so close that she could smell his rotting teeth.

She could not move. Her back was pressed against the wall. She had no escape, so she pointed to the entryway. "Then open that door and go forth to proclaim the new Order. I shall face any required penance as God demands." Even as she spoke, she knew he would fail to take the suggestion. At least it had gained her a few more breaths of life.

"Oh no! There is a crime that must yet be solved, and you shall do so." He chortled. "Not as you thought, but as you deserve instead!"

This time, Eleanor really shivered. She could not run around the man. She had only the wall and window at her back.

He spat in her face. "You shall jump from the window, whore of Satan, because you lusted after your cousin and killed his wife out of jealousy."

"Untrue! And you cannot allege something for which there is no proof!"

"Ah, but there is, for I am the witness to your confession. You called me here to admit your depravity, but you are so devoted to the Prince of Darkness that you could not accept any penance I demanded. Instead, you jumped from that window and killed yourself."

Eleanor suddenly noticed that Sister Serena was struggling to her feet. Her first reaction was to shout a warning to the nun but doing so would mean the girl's immediate death. Was there a chance the nun could unbolt the door and flee for her life? She chose to give the girl that slim opportunity and continued to distract Vincent.

"I will not jump voluntarily, and if you try to force me, I shall scratch and bite you enough to draw blood. That will

199

bring sufficient doubt that I leapt of my own accord. I have been here long enough that your story would not ring true to those who have been in my flock and among my friends." She stiffened into a defensive posture, even though her feigned ferocity was ridiculous for a woman of her size.

Sister Serena had managed to stand and was inching her way toward the fireplace behind Prior Vincent.

Eleanor stopped herself from waving her hand at the nun to go to the door instead and escape.

"It won't matter whether you go out the window alive or dead," the man said. "I will kill you if you do not jump now."

"You could not explain how a woman had killed herself with a knife and then, as a corpse, leapt from the window."

"Quite simply. We struggled, you drew this knife, and I failed to wrest it from you. You stabbed yourself and fell backward through the window."

Eleanor moved a step toward the window so Sister Serena was better hidden behind the man. Did either of them have any chance at all? None for herself, she realized. So which would give the young nun more time to escape, she wondered. Should she jump to her death or fight Vincent over the knife until he stabbed her?

Vincent lifted the weapon, clearly savoring the moment of killing. The blade glittered in the light from the fireplace.

Behind him, Sister Serena lifted the fire fork from the hearth.

With preternatural force, she swung it at the prior.

Blood spurted from Vincent's head and stained the rushes as the man fell face-first onto the floor. He was motionless.

Eleanor ran to the door and unbolted it.

Brother Thomas stood just outside, his hand raised to knock.

33

Brother Thomas poured Eleanor a goblet of wine. Ralf gestured at some food, suggesting that it might also help her regain her strength, but the monk shook his head.

Sister Anne directed Eleanor to her chair in the audience chamber and firmly pushed her into it. "The wine is watered. The chair is obligatory since you might faint attempting to remain on your feet. Do not argue. You have just escaped with your life!"

Eleanor took the proffered goblet. "How is Sister Serena?" Then she sipped and winced. "You claim this is watered wine?"

The sub-infirmarian took the goblet and held it until she decided Eleanor needed another drink. "She will recover. I personally tucked her into a soft bed in a quieter part of the women's side of the hospital. A lay sister will sit by her until I deem the brave girl sufficiently healed not to require full attendance." She smiled. "Her scalp was cut on the wall when her head struck it, but the bleeding stopped soon enough. Her head hurts fiercely, but a little infusion of willow bark will ease that."

"So she is awake. Does she recall anything?" Eleanor did not argue when her friend handed her back the goblet and gestured for her to drink.

"Considering the blow on her head, her memory is understandably vague, but she is surprisingly alert about a few details. She recalls the prior turning toward her and shoving her hard against the stone. She thinks he pushed her by her head but isn't certain."

"How could she have recovered enough to rise as she did and have had the wits to find the fire fork, let alone swing it with enough force to fell him?" Eleanor took a very small sip before handing the wine back with a nod to the sub-infirmarian.

"She does not remember that at all," Sister Anne said. "The first thing she recalls is looking down at the fallen prior and not understanding how that had happened. Her next memory was seeing Brother Thomas kneeling by the unconscious prior and how you took her into your arms and soothed her. She wept, she said, but didn't know why, although she said she felt an immense feeling of peace. She assumed that was because of your gentleness to her."

"Comfort, perhaps, but peace?"

"Her memory of Ralf's arrival or mine is spotty. She knows I examined her and took her to the hospital. She does not recall that I examined the prior or that Ralf had him carried away to be locked up."

"I regret she did not kill him," Ralf muttered. "He belongs to Church judgment, and they won't hang him. Meanwhile, he sits in your comfortable jail cell having gotten the benefit of Sister Anne's fine medical care and bangs on the door or screams to his heart's content while enjoying Sister Matilda's good cooking."

"Yet there is a burly guard outside that door with a cudgel big enough to pound him into bits if he wants to escape," Brother Thomas said. "And Vincent is no longer prior at Tyndal."

"Sister Serena could not have lived with herself had she killed him, Ralf," Eleanor said. "As for his punishment, I do not know if the man is mad or just a vicious killer. The line between the two may be thin. In either case, I wonder if spending the remainder of one's life alone in a windowless cell is so kind. Hanging brings a swift end to life and an earlier judgment face-to-face with God. Living more years in dark silence with growing dread of Hell might bring greater terror. If he is not mad now, he soon will be."

"Some criminals I regret hanging," he replied. "This one I would have found joy in watching as he strangled on the rope. He murdered your cousin's wife and her priest for nothing more than fear of losing the power he had gained here—perhaps even more than any fear of being hanged for the other killing he did. And he tried to murder you and likely Sister Serena as well. I have failed to discover even a dust mote of mercy in my heart for this cur."

Eleanor replied with a gentle smile. "Because of that loving concern for the two of us, Ralf, I shall ask God to forgive more of your sins, although He has long seen through your stern exterior. Had Vincent died in many other ways, I might feel as you do, but Sister Serena showed a remarkable bravery, saved both our lives, and would have gone mad herself with guilt if she had been the one to kill the man. She should not suffer for her courage and life-saving act. Adult men agonize enough from killing in battle. She is still a child."

He nodded, then surrendered to the temptations of the food sitting on the table near the ewer of wine and went to tear off a large hunk of bread.

"I keep thinking back to her strength when she struck the villain down," Thomas said as he grinned at the munching crowner. "How was this possible? She is a tiny and very timid creature and has never exhibited cleverness. Surely his blow would have dulled what wits she has. A sweet nun, as we all know, and hardly an Amazon warrior."

"I can only point to examples, Brother," Sister Anne said. "Sadly, I cannot slip inside any person's soul and see what is actually happening. But I knew a woman as frail as our nun who saw her husband lying under a huge horse which had died and fallen on him. He was suffocating and could not escape. He later said that she put her arms under the horse and literally flipped the beast over him. Then she carried her husband into the village, where his broken bones could be set. Others witnessed her arrival with her large husband in her arms, his hands and feet dragging on the ground. The wife could not explain any of it and gave all credit to God. Her immense strength vanished, and she could no longer lift any heavy things again. Her husband went back to helping her, but without the occasional grumbles he had uttered before."

"But that sense of peace she mentioned," Eleanor said. "That is a feeling that comes from deep in the soul. We all might feel comfort from a gentle act or gratitude for a kindness, but peace is God's gift."

"Then God may have given her two blessings," Sister Anne said, "and since she owns such a tender soul, He may have decided it was the right time to grant both peace and comfort."

Eleanor fell silent as her three friends began to discuss details of the recent events with which she was very familiar. While they did, she let her thoughts remain with Sister Serena.

She had been so impatient with the child and often held her in contempt for her awkwardness and inability to do anything without assistance or excessive guidance. Unfairly, she had compared her to both Gytha and Gracia, who excelled most mortals in wits and competence. Yet Eleanor realized there must be much hidden within the girl. So far, the only hint to that she had gotten from the young nun was the vague explanation that she had left the world for a priory, not because she had a strong vocation, but because the world terrified her.

Eleanor looked down at the rushes under her feet. Despite everything, when the girl was faced with violent death, she had chosen not to escape to save herself, but to remain and strike down a killer who was so much stronger than she—and to do so with clever stealth and amazing strength. Had God done this, not her? Or had He simply freed her to use a force even she did not know she owned?

Despite the many questions she had about Sister Serena, and all she resolved to learn about her, Eleanor knew she must first assure the young nun that she had a secure place in service to her prioress. This would not only comfort the child but allow her to gain the young nun's confidence. Being the timid creature Sister Serena was, Eleanor knew of no one in the priory flock who was friendly with her or even noticed her. Perhaps the older lay sister did, who seemed so willing to help when needed, but that seemed to have been born of maternal kindness, not mutual respect or friendship.

Deep within this child, she said to herself, is an unhealed wound. Priests dealt with sins and cured souls of evil. God often left the healing of other injuries to mothers, and if one did not have one any longer, then a mother must be found. Sister Beatrice took on that role for me, Eleanor thought. It seems that I might have to do the same for Sister Serena.

Eleanor sighed. She might owe her life to this child, but she also suspected that God had sent Sister Serena for another reason. She doubted it was just to teach her tolerance or even to save her life. She suspected it was to teach her something far more profound. With Sister Gracia, a child abandoned to the dark streets and even darker abuse, Eleanor had provided a safe place and love. But Gracia had always had inner strength and was capable of surviving wars, plagues, and individual human bestiality. Sister Serena needed far more protection, and Eleanor knew she must find out exactly what was required.

34

Mistress Megge was helped down from her horse by one of the armed men who had made the trip from Norwich safe for the family.

Her two sons had already leapt from the mounts they shared with household servants and raced to meet her. They competed with each other in shouting their excitement over riding all the way from home on horses, not in carts "like babies". Her weary expression suggested her journey astride a horse had been rather less thrilling, but she smiled at their happiness and planted a kiss on the top of each head.

Brother Thomas approached and bowed to her in respectful greeting.

The boys ran into the snow with shrieks of joy and were soon making great balls of it to fling at each other.

"They love to play in snow, Brother, but little ever remains on the ground in the streets of Norwich for them to have their fun." She looked at him with an expression that blended pleasure in the gaiety of her boys with an ill-defined sorrow. "Did you play like this with your brothers or friends when you were a lad?"

Thomas rarely thought of his youth, and when he did, it

was often with a pang of recalled loneliness and an unpleasant awareness that he was not quite like other boys. That he was a bastard was not what made him different. In his father's castle, there were many of similar birth who had been casually produced by men who served his own father. Instead, it was a growing knowledge, especially as he grew into his teens, that he looked to men for bonding and with lust while others were starting to gaze at women for the same. They were free to jest about this, disguising their deep need with rude mockery. He instinctively remained silent or mouthed a few phrases to sound like others. Later, he even lay with women because that was expected. The physical release felt good, but that was all it ever was. Only with his friend Giles did he feel some fulfillment—until that relationship ended in tragedy.

"You look lost in memory," Mistress Megge said with some tenderness.

"I was," he replied with a short laugh. "You have taken me back to my boyhood." He looked out at the children laughing and shouting creative insults at each other as they warred with affectionate competition. "We didn't have much snow on the ground in London either."

Then silence fell between them, but it was an easy one. He now felt a kinship with Mistress Megge. Both suffered sorrow. The causes were alike—and yet not. Instead of dwelling on this as he had in the past, he brought the Anchoress Juliana's earlier words about the nature of love to mind.

"Your husband has been looking forward to seeing you and his sons. I cannot tell you how much he has missed you and how often he speaks with pleasure of your next visit," Thomas said.

She blinked. "How is his health?"

"Improved. Sister Anne is pleased. It seems her foul

mold is beginning to win the fight against his rotting wound. He reeks less of decay, and there are clean new scars. Although he complains about sudden sharp pains and itching, she says that suggests there is healing. Recent examinations by the hospital lay brothers have not revealed anything troubling." He shrugged. "She does not know why the itching or pain happens, but in your husband's case, these are good symptoms."

"My husband lives in a place devoted to God," she replied. "That is the best medicine of all."

"And he is surrounded by the daily prayers of all our monks and nuns directed to Him at the command of our prioress."

She lowered her head and murmured reverent thanks.

"He is not yet able to take much exercise," Thomas continued, "but he is determined to walk as far as the priory beehives when the weather permits. I have moved the chair from his bedside to the door of his chamber. Sometimes he can reach it, albeit with assistance."

Her expression grew somber. "That is little more than he could do when he was with us in Norwich."

"Both you and I knew any progress would be a miracle and slow at best, mistress. Like you, I would wish for more, but it pleases me that he shows new determination. The trip to see the hives was his own idea. Might not that, plus the improved healing of his wound, be cause for hope?"

She smiled, but the expression held no joy.

Thomas longed to reassure her that Durant was indeed improving, but he suspected tales of how he and her husband had laughed together or how Durant had regained pleasure in life just by holding on to Thomas's arm would not bring undiluted balm to her heart. At least he knew the desired relief was coming soon when she could be alone with her husband. In the meantime, Thomas chose to ease her worry in another way.

"Sister Matilda would like a word with you if you have time today. She runs our priory kitchen and has been trying to tempt him with appealing meals. He speaks often and fondly of your cook. Sister Matilda hoped that you might give her some direction about foods he likes." Rarely did this nun ever ask for advice on cooking. Rarely did she have to. But Brother Thomas decided that it would bring the vintner's wife pleasure if she thought the nun needed her to do so. When he had explained how he wished to handle this issue to Sister Matilda, she had been very willing to support his approach should Mistress Megge come to her.

"Of course, Brother! I know his favorite recipes." Mistress Megge looked genuinely pleased.

As they came to the building where her husband now lived, Thomas stopped so the boys could catch up with them. Before they swarmed over their mother with the youthful enthusiasm that peaks in children just before they fall into sleep from exhaustion, he had one more thing to say to her.

"Coming here for the health of his soul has brought him comfort, mistress. He asked that a small altar be set up in his room where he could see the cross at all times."

A look of relief flashed across her face.

"When I visit, we spend most of the time praying for guidance. I speak less as God seems to be answering his personal pleas for understanding. The solitude in this holy place has brought him a spiritual peace. Your agreement, when he told you of his wish to come here, was a blessing, mistress. The separation must be cruel, but you gave him a gift that most wives would not. He knows it and praises you the more for your sweet and loving kindness."

For a moment, Thomas thought she might burst into

tears, but, as he was learning, she was a woman possessed of much strength. Instead, she crossed herself and looked heavenward as she swallowed all trace of weakness.

Nonetheless, he believed he had provided her with reassurance that her husband treasured her as his wife and helped push further back any fears that he was a threat to her rightful position in her husband's heart. Mistress Megge was a good woman and deserved contentment. In his own heart, he was more secure in the knowledge that the love Durant felt for his family in no way diminished the deep bond and love he felt for the monk.

When they reached the door to Durant's chamber, he opened it to let her in. A lay brother stood next to the vintner and helped him to his feet when Mistress Megge entered. He heard a cry of happiness as she hurried to her husband.

Durant shot Thomas a quick look of love and gratitude, then turned with a joyful and welcoming expression to his wife as he opened his arms to embrace her. The sons hesitated, then each carefully wrapped himself around a separate paternal leg.

Thomas did not wait for the attending lay brother to leave so the family might have time alone. He immediately turned around and walked outside toward the hospital, where he would spend some time with the dying and sick. As he did, he looked toward the anchoress's window. A line of villagers and pilgrims waited their turns to approach and ask her advice.

He smiled and silently sent her a message of thanks for the wisdom she had brought him. Knowing how complex love was gave him comfort. No one aspect had to be in competition with another.

For no reason, he grabbed a handful of snow, formed it into a ball, and flung it as far as he could. Watching the white object fly across the gray winter sky, he felt an odd sensation, something he had rarely felt in his life.

He was happy.

Author Notes

This year began with profound sadness for many of us. Our beloved Sharon Kay Penman died on January 22, 2021. Her death is a terrible loss not only to the historical fiction genre, but to her countless fans and friends. All of us know her status as a giant in medieval historical fiction, but a few might not have known what a truly gentle soul she was. She passionately cared for all God's creatures—with the exception of a few truly monstrous humans—with immense generosity and compassion. It seems that the only time she ever hesitated on this compassion was when a massive horde of ants invaded her kitchen. She struggled to figure out how to discourage them without resorting to the lethal. For the record, she succeeded.

If you have not yet read her work, please start. She wrote "big books", of which she was a master. Her pacing moves with fluid grace. The prose is eloquent, witty, and utterly without pretension or pointless verbiage. Her tales are told with the skill of a Welsh bard, a long-lost art that is a joy to see so skillfully recaptured. Her characters (the good, bad, minor, and major) are three-dimensional. It was a shock to discover, for instance, that even King John had one or two touching virtues. And since Sharon was a meticulous researcher, there is excellent reason to believe he did.

My favorites of her work tend to be those with subjects most don't write about. I began with her Welsh trilogy, the first volume being *Here Be Dragons*. Another is her book about the Stephen/Matilda wars, *When Christ and His Saints Slept.* Her last book, *The Land Beyond the Sea,* deals with the little-told tale of what happened in the Holy Land after King Richard went home and the only Franks left were mostly those who had settled permanently in the Holy Land. Riveting tale. Compelling characters. And how can anyone not weep over Baldwin the Leper King, who showed so much courage and died so terribly young, fully aware of his fate?

These are just personal favorites. Being one of her ardent fans, I have eagerly read everything she wrote, more than once, and never found a book to disappoint. Just check out her subjects—and she also wrote four medieval mysteries—then pick according to interest. You are in for a rare treat.

There has never been an Earl of Ness. As mentioned in the past, I try to avoid most real people as performing characters in my books and attempt not to accidentally insult anyone's innocent ancestors. But as you have probably suspected, I couldn't resist "Ness". Being a loyal fan of the Loch Ness monster, I decided his/her homeland deserved a nice earl to rule over it and keep any medieval tourists quiet at night so the sweet monster could sleep. Prioress Eleanor's cousin surely shared my belief that Nessie is real and must be well served.

In the broader historical picture during the time of this story, the Welsh were crushed, although their rebellion never quite ended. Prince Llywelyn was killed in December 1282, which did much to cripple the Welsh effort since he had been the heart and spirit of the cause. His brother Prince Dafydd fled into hiding, but he and his family were captured in June 1283. In August, the conquest of Wales was sufficiently advanced that Edward returned to England.

Until the following spring, the king spent his time touring England for victory celebrations and grand holiday feasts. With improved weather, he went back to Wales and concentrated on spending vast amounts of money building many castles.

Unfortunately, he also did something else rather significant before going off for celebratory hoopla. Instead of hanging or chopping off the head of Prince Dafydd in October 1283, he turned to a form of execution apparently first used by King Henry III for people of lower rank: hanging, drawing, and quartering. I won't provide details of this. Readers are probably quite aware of them, and I find it all sufficiently barbaric that I cannot stomach describing the method. Even the Earl of Ness, a former crusader and experienced soldier, was horrified. He was not alone in that reaction.

Let it suffice to say that Prioress Eleanor had good reason, when her cousin told her about the execution, to fear the results of escalating brutality which gave this form of death penalty a ghoulish legitimacy. Instead of vanishing after satisfying King Edward's pique, the method took hold and was used against many more of all ranks, often for far lesser reasons than exerting independence against an especially prickly English king. And so, as such unsavory things often do, the penalty remained an option for centuries. The last person to suffer it was in 1782, a Scotsman convicted of being a French spy. Two Irish Fenians were condemned to that execution in 1867, but at least the sentence was never carried out. In 1870, the practice was finally officially abolished. Other forms of the death sentence were pretty much junked in the UK in 1965 and the rest by 1998. A wise decision in my always less than humble opinion because, no matter whether one is pro or con the death penalty, it is true that juries do get things wrong, and if the facts later prove the executed people were innocent, there is no way to bring them back from the dead.

In that same otherwise convivial chat between cousins, I mentioned Mary of Woodstock and her parents' reluctance to enclose her as a nun in the Order of Fontevraud at Amesbury Priory. She was the child born to Queen Eleanor in 1279 when Prioress Eleanor was also at Woodstock, praying beside her father's deathbed in *Land of Shadows*. Mary's parents did not want to put her into a convent before she was old enough to know what that meant, but in 1285, the six-year-old girl was delivered to Amesbury Priory to keep her grandmother, Dowager Queen Eleanor of Provence, company when the latter chose to retire there. The child, like her parents and siblings, seems to have had a mind of her own as she grew up and might have been a handful. In later years, her father, brother, and even nephew paid her gambling debts. She also had a comfortable income during her lifetime, which allowed her to spend little time behind walls and much more at court and in other travels. After her death in 1333, the Earl of Surrey alleged he had had an affair with her, a story that has been reasonably debunked.

An interesting small detail. In the medieval period, the North Sea had several other names. It was also known by various forms of the "German Ocean", "Frisian Sea", the "Western Sea" by the Vikings, and "the Dead Sea". The latter apparently reflected the stillness of the water where patches of fresh water formed a layer over the salt water. For clarity, I have chosen to use North Sea in the entire series since it was also used in the thirteenth century.

As you know, I often include things not usually brought to light in works of historical fiction or, until relatively recently, most non-fiction. I don't do this as a plot gimmick. I do it because I find whatever it is worth reminding us that our ancestors shared many of our questions and concerns.

(We may find them ignorant or wise, just as our descendants will judge us.) In this spirit, I created Father Fithian, who was intersex, or, as the gender was known in medieval medical and religious texts, a hermaphrodite. This term is not used today, but I could not use "intersex" in a historical book.

The idea was born when I found myself wondering why so much time is spent today attempting to shove the definition of gender into a perfectly round hole when it isn't an even shape of any ilk at all. The question of identity has always been a far more complicated question than many think or recall. Ask a teenager, for instance, how important as well as how difficult a process it can be. For anyone born physically or even psychologically intersex, it is far harder, especially in societies that insist on confusing artificially constructed social rules with reality.

Society's "rules" defining the roles of men and women not only vary from culture to culture but often include the misconception that there are only two physical genders. Instead, there are at least three biological ones: male, female, and blended. And if we have proof that observably physical gender can be blended, then what is the problem with people intellectually crossing over many arbitrarily constructed boundaries so they can function as happier and more productive members of society? It is a fallacy to say that a woman "thinks like a man" or that a man "behaves like women", both usually intended as insults. In another culture or era, all gender identifiers may be differently defined. There is no crime in defining oneself as one is, not as one is expected to be.

So how did the medievals deal with those who were physically intersex?

As I browsed through writings on the subject, I was surprised to discover that they didn't react in quite the way many of us might have expected. The medievals were fully aware that humans were created in three biological genders: female, intersex, and male. That said, they also believed that humans could only be female or male because that is what God had created in Adam and Eve.

Quandary!

And thus, after considerable and detailed discussion, rules were created. A medieval child born as intersex was usually assigned a male or female gender close to birth. Occasionally, this decision was delayed, and individuals could sometimes choose for themselves. Once this decision was made, it could not be changed except in extremely rare situations and then usually from female to male. Males were, after all, deemed to most perfectly resemble God and were the preferred gender designation.

Once gender was assigned, the person dressed, acted, was trained, and had the legal restrictions and occupational choices/prohibitions of the chosen gender. Therefore, Father Fithian could become a priest if he had been assigned the male gender. Marriage was possible between an intersex person assigned one gender with a non-intersex person of the opposite gender as long as the prospective spouse didn't mind that person had at least rudimentary male or female genitalia. Children were born of these unions unless, as in the case cited by Sister Anne, it was physically impossible. The other prohibition was that an intersex person must use the genitals of the gender assigned, even when they didn't "work" but the other genitals did. To use male genitals if assigned "female" or vice versa was to commit the sin of sodomy.

Changing assigned gender, as previously mentioned, was prohibited in almost all cases. This seems to have been the problem with Father Fithian. It appears that he had been assigned a male gender but briefly acted as a woman when he fell in love with the unnamed crusader. As a man, he could become a priest, something for which he clearly had a true calling. But if he changed gender assignment even once and that became known, he would have been banned from the priesthood and condemned as a sodomite. His fears were real, and he had good cause to be terrified that Eda would reveal his secret.

Not to say that there wasn't prejudice against those born intersex. Many inside the Church and in the secular world condemned them as wicked and vile. But there at least was some attempt to integrate them into a two-gender world without violence or bigotry. My characters were also not unusual in asking how God, who was perfect, could have created a "creature in His own image" that was less than perfect in the common view. I suspect Brother Thomas may well continue to ponder the questions swirling around an intersex person along with his fellow churchmen, but his unspoken thoughts are also likely to go far deeper.

Because less of grand historical note was going on, and I have already written a book about the effect of the Welsh wars on my group of monastics in *The Twice Hanged Man*, there are fewer new resource books this time to mention. I have listed some generic works again for those new to this series. Instead, I chose to center this mystery more on Prioress Eleanor's family. That was needed for the day when I hope to deal with any murder that might take my prioress to Scotland when King Edward I gets bored beating up on the Welsh and switches to the Scots. He may have been best known for being "the hammer of the Scots" when he died, but I think he did much more hammering of the Welsh before he moved on to new prey in the north. That statement would likely find agreement with my Welsh ancestors.

A Great and Terrible King: Edward I and the Forging of Britain, by Marc Morris; Windmill Books, 2008.

Armies of the Crusades, Men-At-Arms Series, by Terence Wise; Osprey Publishing, 1999.

Eleanor of Castile: Queen and Society in Thirteenth Century England, by John Carmi Parsons; St. Martin's Press, 1998.

Knight of Outremer 1187-1344 AD, by David Nicolle; Osprey Military Warrior Series 18; Reed International Books,1996.

Meanings of Sex Difference in the Middle Ages, by Joan Cadden; Cambridge University Press, 1993.

Framing Medieval Bodies, edited by Sarah Kay and Miri Rubin; Manchester University Press, 1994.

The Very Secret Sex Lives of Medieval Women, by Rosalie Gilbert; Mango Publishing, 2020.

BOOKS BY AUTHOR

ACKNOWLEDGMENTS

Donis Casey, Peter Goodhugh, Patrick Hoi Yan Cheung, Maddee James, Henie Lentz, M. Louisa Locke, Paula Mildenhall. Sharon Kay Penman, Jenny Quinlan, Marianne Silva, Lyn and Michael Speakman, Judith Starkston.

ABOUT THE AUTHOR

Priscilla Royal has written seventeen books in this thirteenth century English series, featuring Prioress Eleanor and Brother Thomas of the famous Order of Fontevraud. This book is Priscilla's most recent. Her website is www.priscillaroyal.com.

Made in the USA
Columbia, SC
19 September 2023

23095036R00140